Brightwill

Randolph Lalonde

BRIGHTWILL
Smashwords Edition
Copyright (c) 2014 by Randolph Lalonde

Cover titling and design by Randolph Lalonde.
Internal sketch work by Marcus Froment
Ebook formatting by Jesse Gordon.

Special Edition "Brightwill Illustrated" ISBN: 978-0-9937398-4-2
Print ISBN: 978-0-9937398-3-5
EBook ISBN: 978-0-9937398-2-8

BRIGHTWILL

Chapter I

"The morning routine gets longer as I grow older," Master Naze Kinu said as his minder finished straightening his long summer robe. The grey and white garment was light and loose, a mercy in the impending heat of the day.

"You are young yet, Master Kinu," said Doril. Every day the man started by addressing him formally.

Every day, Naze told him, "By my first name, please," and today was no different. "Let's move to the window."

He stepped down from the short dressing block and walked to the window, his left knee creaking. Doril picked up the box, carried it to the window, and motioned for Naze to step up. He did so, deciding to forgo his regular objection. Naze never saw the necessity for the box, Doril no taller than he, and he didn't need the help in noticing flaws in the way his clothing adorned him. Given the choice, Naze would do away with the fuss of straightening and adjusting altogether. Physical perfection was a goal for dreamers and preening ladies.

Doril was only two years junior to Naze, and they had been lovers for a time two decades before. If anyone had earned the right to dispense with formality, or to encourage his employer to dress himself in the morning, it was he.

There were even whispers in the halls of the Amber Refuge that Doril would be the next Keeper of the Light if Naze ever retired or died. He felt his seventy-seven years, there was no doubt, but retirement wasn't a part of his plans. Just as importantly, Naze knew he hadn't reached the end of his potential, even at his advanced age. Even still, time was very limited; that was an important thing to keep in mind.

Naze straightened his shoulders and gazed through the open arch as Doril opened the shutters. The cool morning air gave him a chill, and he smiled. The yellow sun fought to cut through the mist on the horizon. Strands of black smoke rose in the distance, still too close for Naze's liking, but farther than yesterday. The shadows in Dolosi were still long. Breakfast was just about to be served in the hall three floors beneath him.

Naze looked through the window to the courtyard as Doril tugged a side section of his robe straight. The paving stones and supports were formed from mountain rock, carved with the power of gifted magi. He was one of the people who worked the stone using the Stone Path, an elemental focus of the Light, a school of discipline he had been teaching for decades. He remembered building his sections of the place, telling the rock to become a bit of paving here, or an arch there. The grand, circular courtyard he looked into from his window was finished in three months instead of three years. All but one of the magicians who constructed the Amber Refuge were still alive, several of them still served. It seemed like it was so long ago, but his thoughts were drawn back to an even earlier time in his life by something he saw then.

A young student with shaggy blonde hair climbed a column as though he were a spider on a web, leaping over the railing on the floor above and running towards the dining hall. "That one might be too late for his breakfast this morning," Naze muttered with a chuckle.

"Would you like me to have something said to his master? Tardiness is a poor habit," Doril said as he picked up a new over cloak. The material was gossamer thin in all but the middle, where silver and golden thread scrollwork decorated the collar and a strip running down the front.

"No, his hunger is more than enough punishment," Naze said. "It was punishment enough for me."

"By the way, happy birthday," Doril said as he finished gently lowering the over cloak onto Naze's shoulders. The smile made the man look twenty years younger.

"Thank you," Naze said, "who else knows?"

"That this is your birthday?" Doril asked. "No one, I know how you hate being celebrated."

"We should celebrate each other when we can, every day," Naze said. "Why should the day I was born be any different?"

"You could take some time, relax for a change," Doril said. "Visit the Wayists. Kovak hasn't had the opportunity to show off his students for months."

"I'm afraid I already have a day planned." He had been secretly looking forward to his birthday for months. A plan he had been pursuing for decades would come together after risking friends, talented students, and his own life more than once. Many knew that he had been planning, preparing, gathering the rarest of articles and taking long journeys. They suspected that it was all for a masterwork, some great feat that consumed decades of his life.

Many asked him what his goal was over the years, and he'd told only who he had to, only people who were there at the very beginning. Anyone who knew him stopped trying to get hints at what his masterwork would be. Over the years, people had plied him with liquor, shared precious intoxicating herbs with him, and even dangled other tantalizing prospects in front of him in efforts to pry his secrets loose. Naze gladly allowed himself to be boozed, intoxicated, and occasionally seduced over the years, but was very proud that he never let the nature of his masterwork slip. The bribes were a cost his friends and enemies paid as a lesson – you couldn't pry secrets loose from that master wizard, no matter what expense you went to. He made sure to thank whoever was offering those briberies, just the same.

His birthday didn't normally mean much to him, and he hadn't celebrated it for many years, but this one, his seventy-seventh, would be different. He considered it a marker in time, the first such occasion when all the knowledge he needed had come together so he could finally perform his masterwork. Nineteen rites had been conducted leading up to the date, the appropriate gifts had been given to the masters of magic and men, and he'd prepared himself as best as he could. There was one more thing he felt he had to do before the masterwork could take place. "I'm going to tell stories about my brother today."

Doril stopped straightening his over cloak for a moment. "You've never spoken of him before, there are lessons in his story?" He gestured for Naze to step back up onto the block.

Naze obliged and Doril continued to straighten the finicky middle piece to the garment. The metal thread was kinked in a few places. "There are lessons. I'm sure many things I tell students about him today will be useful to them, but it is how I'm celebrating my seventy-seventh. So many years for one life, so many of them passed in his absence. It's time to reflect, and to honestly assess the direction in which I'm taking things."

"What was he like, your brother?" Doril asked.

"I knew you'd ask," Naze said.

"You have a story to answer that very question," Doril said, stepping back and smiling at him.

"You know me too well. I'm proud to tell you that I am the fraternal twin to Riv, though few believed us since we looked nothing alike."

"The thief? The goblin?" Doril asked, forgetting all formality, staring up at him wide-eyed.

"The very one, and let me tell you: the moniker of Goblin was well earned, but not in the way you might think. I was glad to observe the deed from the audience."

"Did the people Riv kill and rob deserve it as well?"

"I'm afraid there have been exaggerations in his legend over the years," Naze said with a chuckle. He expected that reaction from his long time companion. The victors always wrote history, and his brother was savagely vilified on the page. "In truth, Riv killed seldomly, the other murders were laid at his feet by people who outlived him, many of whom envied his fame. Even after he disappeared, people told stories about him, his fame, or infamy, depending on who you speak to, only flourished in his absence."

"Even still, all the Ondi know Riv, and there are no shrines for his return for a reason," Doril said.

"Many people have lied about my twin. The truth may not be as flattering as I'd like either, but it's better than what people believe. Today I'll make sure it's known. I'm sure people will learn from him, and people's reactions should be dulled a little more than yours since he's been missing for over half a century."

"You don't need to name him. Tell your stories, honour his memory, but call him by another name."

"How can I honour him with a name he never had? I'm surprised at you, Doril. I thought you would support me above all others." A complete lie. Naze was certain of the opposite, but looking hurt had won him more than one argument with his long time friend.

Doril finished straightening Naze's robe and stood back. The man's dainty, pointed ears were red, a sign of agitation Naze was familiar with. "I want to hear every detail, make no mistake, but should everyone else know about your brother?"

"I need your support today. I need to tell my story to a crowd; they will respond to it and help me decide if my past is properly informing our future. History was kind enough to forget I was Riv's brother, that I owe him everything. Now it's time to repay him, and I need an ally."

"If it were anyone else," Doril said, shaking his head. "But I can't miss the opportunity to hear whatever stories you're about to tell, even though you insist on having an audience. I'll stay by your side, as always."

"Good," Naze said, clapping his hands together. "Now, let me begin by telling you a story that should help you see my brother the way I did. My mother named us together, Rivnaze, after the great dragon of legend, the wise Justicar of the Azure Court. He was Riv, since he was born first. He was the impulsive one, and I was the watchful one.

We were born during happy times, before the Liberation War, but only by a few years. My mother was a healer, named fleshcrafter by humans, even though she only ever laid hands on the injured to mend them. My father was a great shaper of stone, a flame speaker as well, and I never got to see it, but people would hire him to climb the high places and he would sculpt dragon heads, crests for royalty, and all manner of things.

The Children at Play sculpture in the South Yard is the only surviving piece I could find.

"I know, I often stop to admire it," Doril said. "I almost expect one of the figures to run free of their pedestal, they're so life like."

"He included Riv and me in that piece, I'm the one with my hands raised, laughing, my brother is the one chasing me, his hand grasping for the back of my tunic. The other children in the circle were all from our neighbourhood."

"Before the Liberation War," Doril said, his expression darkening.

"I won't go into detail about what happened to my parents," Naze said. He wanted to address those dark days and get them out of the way quickly. Everyone knew the story of the Ondi during that time. "My mother and father, as well known practitioners of magic, were culled during the final nights of the Liberation War. My brother and I were hidden with most of the children until the war was over, and the humans overthrew the old rulers, the Ava-Ondi, then defeated the Monarch Dragons. While my memories of my parents are faint, I do have many memories of the Ondi District, where the Woodlanders were crowded into the poorest part of town. We were educated young, and protected fiercely by the elders, like all the other Ondi-Ne children. That's why they were so disappointed with us when, during our adolescence, Riv and I started taking measures to improve matters in the Woodland District without consulting them.

"That takes me to the beginning of the story I want to share with you about Riv, my brother. On a morning much like this, I was keeping watch from the top of a garden wall as he did something our elders didn't approve of. It's something I'll never regret just the same, especially since it was so very necessary, or at least, we thought it was at the time."

Chapter II

The cool pre-dawn air stirred the scents of the high-walled garden. Imported black earth, the faint smell of Violet Bell flowers and of early morning bread from the nearby bakery filled the air. It was the only distraction my brother allowed himself as he stood as still as a post amongst a stand of tall sunflowers, waiting for a pair of burly guardsmen to pass. The darkness of night was fading, and I so wished they'd move along as I watched from the top of the wall surrounding the massive estate garden. I hugged the top of that stone divide, my cheek pressed to the cool rock as I watched, holding my breath. I was the lookout; my brother, the nimbler one, was the thief.

The sunflowers were more than twice his height, a perfect refuge, and the guards were only a little taller than the flowers. The scant pre-dawn light glinted on the studs on the guards' leather armour and the swan shaped pommels of their swords.

I watched them walk around the bend leading around an old, dry brick wall before I signalled my brother by tapping a small stone against the top of the wall. Riv crept away from the sunflowers and crossed the path. It would be a nice place for a stroll during the day, but no one in the household would allow us to cross the threshold. As displaced woodland people, Ondi-Ne, we would be shoved clear of the stoop so our presence wouldn't lower the house's status in the eyes of other so-called higher ranks of society.

Like me, Riv was short, even for Ondi, well below half the height of an average human-sized door. Back then, we saw that and other traits we inherited as gifts. We were both quick, but he was especially light on his feet, as alert and silent as a cat on the prowl, and trained in the Way since he could walk. I didn't think that was anything special as I watched him make his way across the garden to his quarry though.

He crept along until he managed to make it to the rear garden wall and his big toe brushed something. He looked down and grinned. He ensured the guards were still on the decorative side of the garden. I could see the thicker bodied one looking up to an unnaturally bloomed lilac tree. It was out of season; someone had forced it to bloom regardless.

"Hurry! Dawn's practically here!" I whispered to him. "You already have a pouch full!"

"Hush!" Riv reached down and picked up a round, firm squash and tucked it into the left side of his loosely tied shirt. He detached another from the vine and stuffed it into his pouch, somehow finding room. "I can eat all day on these," he chuckled to himself. A shape farther inside caught his eye and he smiled even wider. "Cucumbers," he breathed as he quietly rushed to the patch where the tubular vegetables lay. Humans pickled the small cucumbers, but they were the perfect size for our people, and a particular favorite.

He had another in the burlap sack at his side in mere heartbeats. He hurriedly loosened his rope belt so he could stuff another down his trousers when his elbow brushed a stone birdbath.

In a blur of motion, he crammed one end of the cucumber into his mouth and stepped under the top of the heavy garden ornament, holding it up over his head with all his strength as he fought to keep the base of the thing from toppling with a foot. "Idiot," I grumbled as I watched the base topple, filling the garden with a resounding clatter.

The guards came rushing around the corner, over thirty paces distant but running with those damned long, tree trunk legs humans were so well known for. "Oi! This is a private garden!" one shouted, his booming voice further disrupting the peace of pre-dawn.

Riv dropped the top of the birdbath and scrambled towards me, where I waited atop the back wall. His mad dash through the garden was made comical by the melons and cucumbers jostling under his clothing. He dashed between the vegetable rows and bound through the berry patch, a cucumber the size of his arm wedged between this teeth.

The guard in the lead had a broad forehead and big, dark eyes. What he had been crossed with in his lineage was anyone's guess, but it was a large creature, making for an ugly, brutish man. Seven-foot-tall men who look like the ugliest end of crossbreeding make for excellent guardsmen, unfortunately.

Riv bit through the end of his prized cucumber, freeing it from his mouth while wasting as little food as possible and turned to face the nearest guard. He tossed it as hard as he could, nearly pitching himself onto the ground. The vegetable spun end over end through the air and struck the brute in the eye perfectly.

He stumbled, the guardsman behind collided with him. Riv had won some time. "Coming up!" he called out to me as he scrambled up the wall.

"Throw the food first!" I replied.

"Get out of my way! It was only a pickle!" the guard behind shouted to his mate as he tried to get past without trampling the garden.

"He hit me in the eye! How would you feel if I poked you with it?"

I've always been amazed at how greater size is rarely accompanied by greater intelligence. That common fact was definitely to our benefit that morning. Riv and I couldn't help but laugh as he hurled himself at the top of the stone wall. I caught his hand and hauled him high enough so he could finish the climb easily, then dropped on the other side myself.

Riv tossed his bag over. I made my best effort to catch it, and a small melon that had spun free from the flap holding the bag closed. It was as though the culinary gods were smiling on me as the bag's strap fell across my shoulder and I caught the melon in one hand. I couldn't help but laugh as I realized that I'd saved all our food. "Did you see that?" I asked.

Unfortunately I didn't have enough time to put the bag down and catch my brother, who somehow expected me to step under him with arms outstretched. I saw no need; he was a trained Wayist, and should have found the fall easy to tumble out of unharmed.

He fell without encumbrance face-first onto the packed dirt of the alleyway and moaned for a moment before slowly getting to his feet. I wasn't entirely sure if he was exaggerating the trauma of his sudden impact with the ground, but I was hesitant to ask if he was all right as I stood holding a melon like a prized trophy.

Riv wasn't impressed. "Thought you were going to catch me, brother," he muttered sourly. From the pulp and seeds splattered across his chest I could see a squash had broken his fall, somehow the smaller melons seemed unscathed.

"You'll heal, breakfast won't," I replied with a shrug.

The garden gate screeched open to admit the pair of guards from within. "Thief!" the taller one cried as he burst into a run.

"Time to leave!" Riv exclaimed as he rushed towards a narrow alley. The damage from the Liberation War years before had forced two tall walls to lean towards each other, so that only the thinnest folk could squeeze through, and we could press through easily enough.

The guards didn't have a chance at pursuit as Riv and I made a quick pace through the route I had scouted earlier. We were home before the market opened that morning.

Chapter III

"I understand the need to steal food," Doril said as they moved down the Amber Seat's private stairs. The stone there, salvaged from the ruined town at the base of the mountain, was framed in hardwood . Naze never liked it, but the back stair was built so the Amber Seat and his people could move separately from the rest of the people in the refuge. It was a response to an attempt on Naze's life twelve years before, one he thwarted personally. When it came to installing a secret set of passages, the stair included, Naze thought it better to let the people who cared for him build it rather than fight endlessly about his safety.

"We were stealing for our people, not only ourselves. Besides, the food we made off with was at the peak of ripeness, the nobles we nabbed it from would have let most of it rot on the ground. As Riv would say, we were pruning with a purpose."

"All right, that still doesn't shed a positive light on anything he did later on. I know I should be patient, you'll get to some detail or anecdote that will do just that, but most people aren't such close listeners."

"You still want me to keep my brother's name out of these stories," Naze said.

"Yes, or only share them with people you've known for years." Doril was near the point of exasperation, something Naze hadn't seen often. The thought that he may have underestimated the animosity that his brother's name still inspired was impossible to ignore. "And why tell everyone about him now? Today? Your audience will consist of some of the most important people in the region, and if you're telling stories all day, it'll take the Vunen Horde to keep them away."

Naze couldn't help but chuckle at the mental image of a group of dignitaries and students holding an army of raiders at bay while he went on telling tales of his later boyhood. "At this point I'll only tell you that I'm recounting these tales because it's time. Holding off a day, or a week, would not be practical. Besides, it's as though I've been holding my breath for fifty years, you expect me to stop now that I've had a little relief?"

"All right, then," Doril said, throwing his hands up. He took the last three steps a little more quickly so he could stand between Naze and the door leading to one of the main hallways. "You're not going to share his name with everyone until the end of the day."

"But the story I plan on telling at noon will surely reveal who I'm talking about without naming him," Naze said with an upraised eyebrow.

"Now you're teasing," Doril accused, wagging a finger.

"I'll keep the name secret until people begin to guess the identity of my brother, and by then, most people will see him in a brighter light than history sheds," Naze said. "And there will be lessons in those stories that the students can learn from."

"Ancestors, guide me," Doril said, rolling his eyes. "Once you've got your mind set on something, there's no stopping you. One more question," Doril asked slyly. "If your brother was in the garden, too far for you to hear his mutterings, how could you know what he said?"

"What details stone couldn't recall for me, I've gleaned from friends and aquaintences who were able to fill in the gaps of my story," Naze said. "A good question though."

"So you returned to the places where these things occurred, interesting," Doril replied. "And had meetings with friends over the years."

"Mostly."

"Mostly?" Doril asked with an arched eyebrow.

"A man at my age has to have earned the right to embellish a litte, even with my memory. For the sake of the story, you understand," Naze replied.

"For the sake of the story," Doril agreed with a smile.

"But you've altered my course, I'll let my audience uncover his name themselves."

They moved silently through the hidden passage, emerging from a locked library cabinet door at the rear of the Brightwill Court private collection room. Another passage opened to them on their left, where Doril spoke to the spirit who volunteered to guard that invisible door. "He'd like to visit the usual spot," he whispered.

"As you wish," a barely audible, ethereal voice replied. They passed through a dusty shelf heavily laden with large books and appeared in the arch of one of the trial room doorways, one of Naze's favourite spots to watch the students in the refuge he founded for the Ondi he could save from the chaos outside.

It only took him moments to settle into his regular place, watching acolytes and Servants of the Stone walk by. If he were to begin training in the refuge as a young man, like all the people he saw walking by, he would be a Servant of the Stone. The mentors would undoubtedly see that he had a supernatural understanding of how the unloving world worked, how even stone was never completely still. To some, like him, everything was malleable. More importantly, there was no limit to the stories stone could tell if you knew how to listen, if you knew how to read its memory.

Naze never had an accepting institution open its doors for him, but he eventually mastered the discipline of stone with the help of many teachers. He branched out into manipulating other parts of the living world from there, seeking greater masters and challenges along the way. All his talents were hard won. It only seemed easy at first.

As he watched the students go by, most of them paying him the respect of momentarily closing their eyes and bowing their heads as they walked by, something that sometimes resulted in collisions, he couldn't help but wonder how different things could have been for him and his brother if they had a place like the Amber Refuge. A place where they would have breakfast in the morning if they were on time, where they could learn about their natural talents without worrying about where their next meal would come from.

Every student had a soft bed, didn't have to be worried about the elements interrupting their sleep, or being robbed in the night or worse. Even their clothing was taken care of – loose tunics and trousers that were tied together with soft string at the waist and up the front. Some wore the single piece long robes, a telling sign that they were from Tetuno, beyond the Wasted Hills. Naze and his people had rescued so many Ondi-Ne, or Forest Folk, from there before their stronghold was overrun by reavers from the Red Coast. Naze could still clearly recall his chief ranger, Matthew, leading a charge against them to buy enough time for him to teleport the two-hundred and ten people from that place. He drew his attention back from the frenzied time; the people of Yarrow Hall were safe, every last one, and in his care.

He enjoyed being on display, as Doril called it. He could get a feeling from the hundreds of students that passed from the dining halls to their mentors and other destinations. Without saying a word, the mass of them could tell him what troubled the student body, how well they felt his organization took care of them, and what their attitude was towards the Refuge's master.

"Your tea," Lonen said as he came through the door with a stoneware cup. He was an ancient fellow who rarely bothered lifting his head up to look people in the eye. The master conjurer was the third cook to lead the brigade in the kitchens at the Amber Refuge, and had held the position for over a decade. "I added dry cranberry, we have an overabundance in storage, judging from the over-long conversation I had with Ebinult. That woman can talk about wheat for weeks, and berries for a season."

"She caught you rooting around for something special for the tea," Naze guessed. Lonen rarely presented him with plain tea, the man was a River Master before he trained as a conjurer, and knew tea like no other.

14

That was the least of his abilities, and he was a mentor to thirty students along with his kitchen duties.

"I offered to re-hydrate some of Ebinult's food before it gets cooked and she just laughs at me," Lonen said, glaring at the tea pot.

Ebinult, one of the greatest conjurers Naze had ever met. To his constant astonishment she was happiest when she was training students to transform matter lacking all nutrition into food. Very few students could accomplish it, but she never stopped trying to teach them through demonstrations. A good thing too, since nearly half of all the food in their storehouse was a direct result of her dedication. It was a constant irritation to Lonen that she insisted on dehydrating the food for longer term storage before he had a chance to even see it. "The last time you tried rehydrating her food was eight years ago," Naze chuckled, "I'm sure she'll take you more seriously if you offer again."

"I've had students practice on her dried fruit instead, an excellent source of jam, and revenge."

"Why didn't I hear about this sooner? I could just imagine the exploding fruit and Ebinult's face at a basket of dried goods being reduced to paste."

"I didn't have to imagine," Doril muttered with a little smile as he accepted a cup of tea from Lonen. "Speaking of food, I'm wondering, why were you and your brother forced to steal it?"

"You've a brother?" Lonen asked.

"Long gone now," Naze said, "but I'm celebrating my birthday by sharing stories about him."

"You high wizards have no end of surprises and stories," Lonen said. "It's no wonder you never stop talking." With the way the man kept his head down, it was impossible to tell if he was being serious or having Naze on. Doril chuckled, which may have been the old conjurer's intention, and by the time the mirth of the moment was receding, Lonen disappeared along with his tea cart, reappearing somewhere in the vast kitchens to command his brigade of cooks and conjurers, no doubt.

Naze cleared his throat and continued. "Why were we forced to steal our food? There's a whole history lesson in that."

"Well, since you're not using names yet, and we're surrounded by students," Doril said as he stepped into the middle of the broad stone hallway. "You three, do you have anything to do right now?" Doril said to three young girls who were chatting across the hall.

They turned towards him as though he was about to give them a scolding, and from his tone, it almost seemed like it. "No, we are waiting for friends so we can go fishing in the North Pass. There they are now," the tallest girl in the group said.

"Fishing can wait a little, Master was about to start telling me about his life during the time of the Treble Law, and you should hear his story."

There was no delay. The smallest of the girls shouted, "Master is telling a story about our grandparents!" down the hallway. "About the rebellion!" Her shrill voice made up for her minuscule stature.

"Best take your place, Master," Doril said as he ushered him into the room behind them.

"Just so you know, I intended to be sharing these tales in the auditorium. I don't intend to be stuck in a lecture room all day," Naze said as he walked to the middle of the semicircle of staged seating. The seats were made of stone and wood, cushioned with a sturdy conjured moss.

"We'll start here, while I pass the word – Master is holding class today," Doril said.

Telling stories was one of the great pleasures of age, and he indulged whenever he could, attaching all his lessons to tales. The tale of the Ondi-Ne Slum, or Woodland District as it was called when he and his brother resided there was one he'd avoided because his time there could not be described without conjuring up memories of his brother. Just then, as he stood in front of many of his students, he was about to talk about that place, those times because he was talking about his brother, counter to his habit of hiding Riv's existence. For the first time in decades he was nervous. He sipped his tangy tea as students filed in. The fisher students were only the first, and by the time the young people, between the ages of six and fifteen summers by his estimation, were settled, the lecture room was full.

Naze shook his head slightly at Doril, who smiled back, well aware that he'd stolen over fifty students from other duties for his Master's story. "I'd best not delay," Naze said, recognizing several faces in the crowd. Among them was one of the oldest students, Contu, a woman in her third decade who came from parts beyond the Void Sea. She was a head taller than everyone there, descended from mountain folk that many called Dwarves, or cave children. Like his own people, her race never grew to human height, but they had the muscle of a human when they were full grown. He'd found her being punished by a slaver, who had hitched her up to his cart instead of his ox, and he was whipping her down an abandoned street.

It was something he put a stop to immediately. The whip in his hands became a vine, tied him, then turned to stone. Wordlessly, Naze took her from the tack and left. She knew who he was, and was more surprised than anyone when she realized that she had great potential as a shaper, just like him. It was a pleasant surprise; she would have been welcome at the refuge even if she had no talent at all.

Contu was one of the most kind-hearted people in the Refuge. She grinned at him, and he began to tell his tale. "It was fifty years ago, and our people, the Woodlanders, or wee folk, the Ondi-Ne, lived under the Treble Law in the Kingdom of Rasson. That treble law dictated that if any Ava-Ondi or Ondi-Ne were found with written material such as magical work or historical records, magical instruments or a blade longer than the palm of their hand, they would be arrested. Their contraband would be confiscated and sent to the Hall of the Law. The Treble Law was strictly enforced by knights, guards, and our human neighbours. My brother and I were seventeen summers old, and dead set on earning our independence from the home we'd had with other orphans since we were small children. My brother was a thief. I had two books and a sheaf of papers I kept hidden, and I suppose I was a bit of a thief too. Suffice it to say, we didn't heed the Treble Law, not at all. My brother even had a hidden collection of blades, and was a Wayist in training, a young martial artist and shadow dancer of growing talent. I had my master as well. " The dropped jaws and rounded eyes amused Naze much more than he anticipated, and he let a chuckle free in anticipation of the shocking statement he was about to make. Casually, he continued by telling them, over fifty of his students, "we returned home after pillaging a highborn human's garden and escaping from the guards."

Chapter IV

We slept in a shared house, where orphans and surrogate mothers and fathers – many of whom lost their children during the Liberation War – were gathered. So many of us were learning the ways of Ondi-Ne magic, or Wayist martial arts, but to the human city guards, we seemed like little more than urchins, poor and subdued.

Neither my brother nor I liked that home very much, so we made a place of our own, where we may not have slept, but we kept the things which we did not care to share. It was built under the Woodland Slum, into the remains of an old paver's hut that people had forgotten. A place no city guard or enforcer had seen in decades. The path leading to it was minded by Ondi-Ne like my brother and me, rebels and a few sympathisers. A tunnel with many small entrances and confusing passages ran under the hillside the Woodland District shared with other slums. That paver's hut had survived an avalanche of hillside and building matter that happened during the Liberation War, when magicians cracked the earth and scorched the sky, fighting for human dominance. It was buried, and we found it when my brother happened upon a crack in the wall of one of the old tunnels. I used what little knowledge of enchantment I had when I was very young to create a hidden door. My master knew of it, even though I thought it was hidden from all but me and my brother, but he let us have our little room under the district. We hid our mother's shawl, our father's belt, and a few collected knick-knacks in a box there along with a few knives, and an old book I kept mystical observations in. I conjured ink from ash, water and a little blood, and wrote with a pigeon feather by the light of a stolen quick amber bauble that would flicker unpredictably.

The section of the hillside all Ondi were expected to live on was called the Woodland District, which was a cruel jest, because our dwellings couldn't have been further from forests if it were in the middle of the East Ocean.

The whole of the slum was built at the bottom of the hillside, downstream from Lowboard, the poorest human district of Ankon, the Capital City. All of Lowboard's worst business flowed downhill, around and under the Woodland District.

Most people in the Woodland District didn't hide; they lived in the open air, or around our own semi-circular town square. On the most fetid hill of slums, the Ondi maintained a garden that filled the middle of the square like a pillar of life. We had no room on the ground, so we unearthed soil and built upward using materials our neighbours discarded. The most steadfast caretakers made their homes inside the structure, and most of the Woodlanders took their turn bringing water from the city fountains three times a day to keep the plants alive.

It was a beautiful sight, but still only produced just barely enough food during most seasons. The bounty my brother and I brought would be enough to finish filling the youngest bellies. While the elders didn't condone theft, they couldn't argue with its necessity.

The Green Tower wasn't the only high structure the Ondi built in our small district. Six more buildings rose above the central one, spread out along our perimeter to guard the Green Tower. The three tallest guarded against the humans of Lowboard, the lower three watched the rest of the city for guards or other commotions that could prove disastrous to us if they overcame our district without warning. Those six towers rose above the stench of the city, looked over the Conquered Valley and the nine castles that stood out amongst the expanse of buildings that extended in all directions.

Despite the ambitious heights of the Green Tower, the rickety lookouts of Lowboard, and the many castle buildings that rose up from the endless city, there were even taller structures. Our water flowed from aqueducts running beneath broad avenues on pillars. The keeps, strongholds, castles, and walled districts all came before them, and they all paled in the grandeur of the High Streets. A misnomer, for certain. You've seen their wreckage in the wastes at the bottom of this mountain, where their tall brick pillars crushed swathes of houses, and the broad brick avenues that crossed the sky came down, to devastate all below during the Cinder War.

When my brother and I were young, the High Streets were still up, still strong, seemingly eternal. The high born and well monied lived up there, above the rabble, above their castles and subjects. Atop those pillars were hidden cisterns, aqueducts, and strongholds where the most prominent houses kept their soldiers and their knights, their wizards and their vaults. Above that they built avenues, upon which they built new houses, and around those houses famous inns, traders, shops and masters plied their trades. My brother and I had never made the ascension, those High Streets were a different world, where everything must be grand, and pompous, and human. We only saw their waste as it tumbled down onto the least fortunate of streets and alleys, and the long shadows the avenues cast. The Ava-Ondi, or Sky Elves, as they were once called before their extinction, built those places with the assistance of the dragons they enslaved. The humans took over once the Ava-Ondi were overthrown during the Liberation War, and they never learned all the secrets of those high places.

Sometimes the neighbouring humans would try to use long ladders and roughly crafted tools with handles so long they'd bend and droop to try and push our towers over, but we were always alert. Ondi-Ne guardians and the humans who sympathized with us would join together, usually in time to counter their attempts.

The houses of the district were mostly built with found materials too, an old human sized breastplate may form the centre of a hut's roof, or the stones from an old, mossy wall could be repurposed to repair a stout home for four. We may have forgotten the woods of our ancestors, but we'd found a talent for using what everyone else found useless, and our district's town square had something that others didn't − life. That brought colour and food into our existence as well as a way to combat the stench of the city around us.

I remember the riot of blues and reds and greens that decorated the multi-levelled wood and stone streets we used to move from place to place. We knew how to sculpt and chisel, and decorated our paths with finely crafted statues that pointed wherever the craftsperson who made it wanted it to.

We didn't lack in talent, but we lacked in all other things. Status in the city, food, numbers, and space. We lived atop each other, or beneath, like my brother and me, and rebellion against the lords who kept us in our small district was hopeless.

To make matters worse, leaving seemed like a foolish notion. In our youth, my brother and I thought that the country of Brightwill was nothing but city, that buildings and roads and castles had swallowed the world whole. The Kings made it well known that they'd walled their woods, and only fools hunted or gathered on their lands. The punishment for poaching was death, torture for foraging so much as a woodland tuber. The rest, we were led to believe, was farmland. To us, the whole of the world had been devoured by purpose, and was off limits.

We had no elders to speak of forests and nature's harmony, though some of us still believed there was something beyond what the Kings owned, and what the lords' people farmed. Every so often, an Ondi-Ne would venture past the city gates, setting out to find the wild places, and they never returned.

People would gather in the towers after wishing them a fond farewell and watch as they disappeared down the main avenue passing over the top of our hill. They would walk down, into the bustling multitude of the streets and, thanks to their comparatively short stature and the nature of those busy places, disappear.

My brother mourned one of those travellers – Liva Naul, an orange haired, spirited, witty girl – who had left not a year before. He was smitten by her, many of the young men were, and she was our age, but she batted her suitors away. She dreamt of travelling and finding new woods, perhaps even discovering the Flying Fields where it was said that dragons still lived free. She collected things she thought might help her along the way throughout her girlhood.

I knew my brother secretly wanted to go with her on the day she left, but he joined me at the top of the North Tower, a tall, rickety wood thing, to watch her leave. That day I found out how very deep love could cut, as my brother, the verbose boy he was, found his silence for the better part of a month.

I've digressed long enough. Suffice it to say, our home was rank in smell, cramped, and lesser in comparison to all others, but it was all we had. We ran through the tunnels underneath our district, meeting none of our fellows along the way.

It was strange; there were people hiding in those tunnels, and we knew where we should find most of them at that time of day. There was no sign of them. We passed the entrance leading to our corner of the tunnels and passed through a hidden passage that led directly into the courtyard of our district.

We passed from that hidden doorway into a thick cloud of dust and smoke. "Maydo! Nauso!" I called as I saw the vague shape of a tall woman with a long brown ponytail beside an older, stout Ondi-Ne with his thick arms upraised. "What's going on?"

"The humans started pushing our west tower down as soon as it rose above theirs. They just started throwing flame at our defenders."

"Naze, join me in holding the structure!" Nauso said, and I didn't hesitate in joining what little power I had at the time with his. As I began to merge I saw where the flames were beginning to take the middle of the roughly built tower, its boards and old branches were easy kindling. Nauso was drawing the fire's elemental power into himself and changing the energy, channelling it into the force he needed to keep our tower upright.

I opened my mind and spirit to him, and Nauso gathered my power into his own. I recall what he was doing with perfect clarity, even half a century later. His will gripped the sturdiest parts of that tower, keeping it upright as humans leaned over with long poles from a shorter tower they'd built uphill. Rarely have I met a more powerful practitioner than

Nauso; he could have turned his will against them and forced them off their perches, or set them on fire, but that was not his way. He believed a day of integration would come between the races and he wouldn't be the one to add a complication.

Our wavering tower was steadying thanks to Nauso, myself, and several of his younger students. Under his direction, I was able to achieve trance-like focus, and I didn't take note of my brother's actions until he was halfway up the teetering tower.

His master, young Maydo who was only ten years his senior, was already busy guiding people from the middle of our tower. She didn't notice as he climbed past her with grace and speed; I've only met one other who can climb the way he did. I didn't think it was so impressive at the time, I was irritated, in fact. I thought he was foolish to climb headlong into danger. He moved with sure grace, hand over hand, swinging, jumping his way up the tower towards the charred upper section with three large water skins looped over his shoulders. He sprayed the blackened wood, ignoring a crowd of humans behind him who were drawing ladders up the tower standing in their district.

"Come down, you idiot!" I shouted. "You'll be killed!"

"Don't stop him, he's helping the people we have trapped at the top come down," Nauso said. "There are only three of them left."

"Be careful! Remember to maintain your balance, no matter what!" Maydo called up to him, "You can't help anyone if you lose it!"

A human three times my brother's height stood atop the enemy tower. Its boards didn't seem much better than what we used, but it was wider. I couldn't help but take note that the man, though massive, looked as poorly dressed and ill-fed as we did. Lowboard was almost as much a slum as Woodland. My sympathy for the man drained away as someone passed him a long pole with a jagged iron hook on the tip. As the humans below him pushed at our tower from their own with long tools and rickety ladders, he began to reach with his hook.

That dreaded instrument was longer than any of the other rough tools the humans pushed and prodded with, and that's saying something. Those instruments of destruction were twenty feet long, sometimes

24

longer, and required two, three, and four humans to hold steady. One of them wouldn't normally do much damage, but the humans crowded on their tower, pushing at our perimeter watchtower with ten poles and a couple of ladders. Such savage destruction still causes me pause, it took time, precious materials and dedication to attack us from one tower to another.

The giant human atop their tower was able to hold and direct his long pole with masterful precision; the hook at the end caught a rope bundle on the second try. Our entire tower wobbled dangerously as he yanked. Many of the humans beneath him on their ramshackle structure cried out in alarm as their tower rocked a little as well.

My brother was busy at work, hastily helping down the three people who were trapped. He took an old instrument from the last one, a tool with a hammerhead on one side and a hatchet on the other. As soon as the last of our friends was climbing down our tower beneath him, my brother, the hero, the idiot, turned towards the giant who wielded a hooked pole. "Oi! I'll be having that!" he shouted as he leapt towards the iron hook.

"Now he's going to get killed," Nauso said.

"Don't get killed!" Maydo shouted.

"Don't worry," my brother called back as he swung around the tower on a length of rope. "I'm your most promising student! What can go wrong?"

"Just because you require more of my time than any other, doesn't mean you're my most promising student!" Maydo retorted as she helped the first of the three my brother had saved down.

My brother had a savage grin on his face as he gripped frayed lines and tried to maintain a foothold on the dancing hook beneath him as he swung his hatchet. The human at the other end of the pole tried to pull his hook free of the ropes and boards. "Get that one! Get that little bastard!" he shouted.

Long tools were clumsily poked and waved in my brother's direction. A roughly sharpened two-tine fork swept at him, others with wooden tips and some kind of ill-constructed scissor-ended thing that seemed to be controlled with ropes all tried to stab, or slash, or knock him down. He swung and shifted out of their way, letting only a light tap from a poker through. The force of it wasn't enough to bother him. He was having little success with his hatchet thanks to all his dodging, so he changed his footing and began to lean towards the giant human's hook.

"Don't you dare," I said under my breath.

As though he heard me, my brother glanced in my direction the instant before letting himself fall onto the giant human's pole, just under where it joined with the giant iron hook. A quick glance at how the twenty-five foot long pole was bowed and where my brother hung from it told me that the situation could only lead to disaster.

"He's clear of the tower, we must begin folding the structure into itself so it falls straight down slowly," Nauso told me and everyone cooperating with the effort.

"But he won't have a way down!" Iss, one of Nauso's students, a little girl with snow-white hair, protested.

"Don't worry about him, he must have an alternate route planned," Nauso replied.

"One that will involve a healer by the end, I'm sure," I replied mentally.

My brother, the hero, the idiot, the would-be legend, did something that I would not have believed if I hadn't seen it myself. He wrapped his legs firmly around the giant human's pole, held fast with one arm, and swung his hatchet hard with the other. Again, again, again, and once more he swung, and to my astonishment, it was enough to dislodge the hooked iron head of that instrument.

Sadly, natural laws dictate that the sudden removal of that great iron weight at the end of the pole will force the wood to straighten and bend in the other direction abruptly. I watched as the pole did just that, flicking him off the end nearly straight up into the air.

His legs and arms were splayed out in the morning light, and I remember thinking that he looked like a frog in mid-flight, except for the panicked look on his face. I swear I could hear his startled shriek from where I stood a couple hundred feet away. He was flung so high, in fact, that he nearly collided with a bird that had been wheeling above with its flock.

I stared in horror and disbelief at what happened next. My brother turned his attention to the situation below, where our tower was slowly collapsing, and the human's tools still reached for it. As though it was his plan all along, he fell, and he tried to catch the first pole he passed, brushed it with his fingertips, and caught the end of the second with both hands. The pole bent, and bent, and his descent slowed until he set both his feet down on the roof of the miller's house as gently as he would if he were descending a stair, then let the pole go. It flicked up into the air as he casually strode to the edge of the roof.

"Moron," I grumbled under my breath, at the same time relieved that luck favoured fools.

Maydo called the retreat. "Everyone move away from the tower! They're bringing it down!"

I felt Nauso begin forcing the upper half of the tower down slowly, crushing the ruined structure into itself. The fire the humans started with flaming pots was long extinguished, and they were retreating, feeling like victors, no doubt.

We were joined in magic, our essences were all attached, and I did my very best to remain calm. It was the best way to make sure my Master's other students could remain focused, clear minded.

My mind was set on following Nauso's unspoken direction. Though gravity was trying to draw the tower to the side, so it would fall across several houses, we forced it back. If we weren't there, many homes would have been destroyed, people would have been crushed. Several of the supports at the base of the tower snapped and the weight increased.

"We have to hurry!" I shouted as I felt Nauso begin to strain. I closed my eyes and lent him my entire consciousness, embracing the blackness that overcame me as I surrendered my very will to our master magician.

I awoke some time later to the sound of masticating. "Naze, you all right?" asked my brother, who seemed far too jovial for the circumstances as he chewed on a bite of melon he really should have finished before talking. "Is there some of my brother left in there?"

"Of course there is," I said as I sat up. We were in Maydo's home, a pair of rooms dug into a large mound with walls made from fired clay, called a potter den. Oroza the Dragonling, an occasional companion to us in those days, was perched on my bedpost. He looked me over with his green eyes, the flecks of yellow in them glinting in the half-light. "He's fine, as I said. Now, stay still while I heal your wounds," he said, turning towards my brother.

He twitched back, holding a hand up between himself and the foot-long dragonling. "I'm not going to be your practice doll, I've seen what happens when a fleshcrafter gets distracted; I don't want to know what happens when their gifts are only a week old."

"I discovered healing power ten days ago now, the better part of two weeks," Oroza said, handing me a small cucumber.

I was grateful for the breakfast Oroza gave me, but I couldn't help but wonder where the rest of our find went, hoping it didn't get lost in the rubble of the tower. "The rest of the food?"

"Gave it to Maydo as soon as the tower was down. Tell me you saw me take that giant's hook before you fainted," my brother said, a little too enthusiastically.

"I did not faint, I gave all my will to Nauso," I replied, "so, no, I didn't see," I lied. I didn't want to acknowledge his idiotic heroics. I may admire him for his bravery now decades later, but back then I thought he was touched in the head.

"Just as well," Nauso said as he entered the increasingly cramped space. "You overextended yourself in your own way, Naze. I'll clap your ears if you ever surrender your will like that again, to anyone."

"Shouldn't you be thanking him?" my brother asked, putting himself between Nauso and myself. He was older by mere moments, but sometimes you'd think my brother was born years ahead of me by the way he'd randomly leap to my defence. "Without him, I doubt you could have kept that tower from going over."

"Stand easy, little warrior," Nauso said with an amused expression, "You're right, you were both heroic in your actions, but equally reckless. We owe you our thanks for joining us in the defence, but I expect both of you to train even harder. You're coming of age, and I know how powerful the will to make a place for yourselves is, but the training you began as children should not stop. This is the perfect time of your lives to grow in the vocations you've chosen. Having said that, there's no training today. The Lord's Guard are already making their way through the city. The humans of Lowboard have reported that you made an attempt at direct combat, and guardsmen are coming to investigate. They'll find that none of us fought humans on the ground, but who knows what will be destroyed as they pick around looking for proof."

"We have work anyhow," my brother said. "Think you can put a day in?" he asked me.

I felt refreshed and rested, a sign that Nauso had restored my spiritual energy with his own, so I nodded, knowing that we had little choice. Strangely, I couldn't recall what sort of work we were supposed to be doing that day, and that was a mercy, as it turned out.

Chapter V

Good work was difficult to come by, especially for Ondi, who were generally viewed with hatred or uncertainty. It only took one generation for humans to circulate vicious tales of Ava-Ondi smothering children in their sleep, or Ondi-Ne luring children into their Secret Wood – if only there were such a thing, I'd have never left – where they would become one of them, or a slave, or be eaten. To adults, we were potential pickpockets, deal breakers, and overall, strange creatures who spoke too quickly and could revolt at any time. What's worse, most of the remaining Ondi-Ne thought humans were lumbering, slow-tongued idiots, who mucked up the sewer systems much more than they ought to by sheer quantity alone.

To be fair, none of those things are true on either end. For the most part, the Ondi don't care to smother children, back out of deals, or lure people away from their homes, though the pickpocket rumour was often true. As for humans, well, they were paranoid about Ondi, because of the Ava-Ondi, or Sky Elves, who ruled over them for so long. It's true that most humans live from moment to moment more than twice as slowly as Ondi-Ne, but that doesn't make them slow witted. Nor were they typically cruel. While I admit that my brother and I had our prejudices - we preferred the rare company of our own kind - we weren't opposed to doing honest business with humans, and we knew several who were very kind.

Our employers that day were not particularly kind, but they had coin, and no reservations about hiring us to do work that was too dirty for most of their servants. Ondi-Ne have the questionable advantage of being small, able to fit where humans have difficulty. Most of our honest work depended on that trait, and I don't recall enjoying any of those jobs. We never found what you would call, 'good work,' only 'honest work' and it was barely enough for my brother and me to keep from resorting from pickpocketing in the market.

As a team, we were excellent pickpockets. It was an opportunity for me to practice box magic, the kind of thing an apprentice could learn in his or her first week, and those distractions were almost always enough for my brother to get his hands into pockets, or his little blade across the purse strings. The challenge would come when we were caught regardless of our talents, and we had to flee.

Stealing from a garden is one thing; it's much easier to plan your escape route in advance, and you can do it at night, when there's no one about. Pickpocketing is an entirely different proposition. We needed people, lots of people gathered together in a market or bazaar, to effectively use our style. Our escapes took advantage of our subject's obliviousness, and when they noticed us at work, we'd use the busy crowd to escape.

We were good at pickpocketing, yes we were, but we had also known enough pickpocketing teams who got caught, and we had become aware of the dominant rule of the trade. No pickpocket has ever retired due to old age. That's to say, every career pickpocket eventually gets caught, and for an Ondi in that kingdom, in those days, that meant the ruling magistrate could do whatever they liked with the caged Ondi.

Thieves were sent to mines, forced to work in the precarious, high places, made to scrape out latrines, repair plumbing from the inside, sold to the arena, and in some cases sold to the dockside slavers of Shir. Palla and Noro, good friends of mine, never came back after they were caught. My brother and I watched the auction where they were sold to a sea slaver for eleven silvers each, and, like I said, I have not seen them since, not in all my travels over these long years.

Even though my brother was tempted to pickpocket, and he mentioned it before we started any disagreeable job, I refused. If he pressed, I reminded him of Palla and Noro, even though I wished we could pickpocket as well. Even sneaking into the home of some lord and stealing away with some silver trinket that would keep us fed for a month was tempting, but I didn't dare mention that to my brother. He'd have at it without consideration of the potential consequences.

I was barely out of the Woodland District when I remembered what dreadful job we had that day: we were to work in an old aviary.

"So, the aviary today?" I asked as we walked through the tunnels running under the district. I knew, but I had to be sure.

"Aye. Lucky the Wrems seem to like us, I guess," my brother stated. The Wrems were an old human family who survived the last war. The seneschal of their house enjoyed using the Underhill Piper, a pub where you'd find mostly Ondi and other little folk, to hire help for jobs that were too low for their human servants. We made many coppers through House Wrem, and I'm sure we saw parts of their keep that they never laid eyes on.

"At least they pay," I replied. "I'm still stinging over the brush off we got from the Autekorkes. Cleaned behind and between every barrel in their cellar and walked away with two bottles of last year's rum for our trouble." I complained more back then, but even so, I had something to whine about. That job took the entire day, and there were five of us. "Then you and Oroza got into my bottles while I was sleeping."

"It was gut-rot, I told you, we did you a favour," my brother protested. "You should move on, today promises to be better. Well, it promises honest pay, anyway."

The street had fully come to life during our short idle time and the exchange with the knights. Shopkeepers opened their stores, workers began making their trek to their posts and the various sounds and smells of the Kinton Market District rose to a din as we left the shelter of a sewer passage. My brother and I made our way to the small castle where the filthy aviary awaited. We knew that market well, and fell in with the rhythm of hundreds of feet. We couldn't see the sky for all the humans that made their way through those pedestrian streets, and most people didn't notice us weaving our way between them.

When we were noticed, people paid us little mind. We were urchins, a pair of poor, ragged folk who wore threadbare clothing and made our own shoes from cuts of discarded leather. The wealthier someone who noticed us looked, the more repulsed they seemed, something I often found amusing. A large woman with shining medals dangling from her knotted hair saw me and nearly knocked into three people trying to get a little more distance from me, and I couldn't help but grin at her with my hands cupped in front of me. Her revulsion became indignation as the crowd parted a little for her. "How dare you beg in the middle of the street!"

To their credit, humans have little difficulty laughing at their own, and she received little sympathy as she disappeared into the throng of pedestrians. "And people think I'm the one who causes trouble," my brother told me as he tugged my sleeve towards Wrem House.

Our journey took us closer to the edges of the street, where we could see the proud storefronts, a view I always enjoyed. I was never one to enjoy commerce or trade, but something about all those shops lined up with hawkers yelling, pretty things on display was mesmerizing. They were up to three storeys tall back in that day. Statues marked some shops, while inlaid carvings and bright symbols along the side of the street called attention to others. Most of the red and dark grey bricked buildings were new. The ones that survived the great quake a decade before weren't quite plumb, a few even leaning enough to create a triangular alley between them and their neighbour. The cobblestone streets in the area had been re-levelled and repaved using rounded stones from nearby creeks and streams.

From where we walked along the street, we could see the broader avenue ahead, where horses - giant creatures to us, especially then when we saw them so rarely - drew carriages or carried the wealthier folk.

It was a parade of the world to me back then. The Market was adjacent to Shir Port, and filled with trades people of every kind. What was imported there was made into useful and desirous objects and sold in the city and beyond. My brother never grew weary of the place.

The glint of several gold rings adorning the hand of a well coiffed man walking across the street caught his eye. It was gone a moment later, but not before I noticed. "Probably fool's gold. Merchants who wear the real thing are rarely afoot in this area."

"Just one of those rings, even in fools gold..." my brother muttered.

"Could land you in the stocks as much as in the room of an inn," I replied.

"A room with two beds for two months if I took a ruby or garnet ring."

He was right, and no one cared that we were Ondi rebels in a human inn. "The stocks," I reminded. "Or slavery, or worse."

"I'm really very good, you remember last year. We had a great time after I caught that drunkard with a heavy purse. Liberating his coins was more of a favour. What he would drink away we lived on from Summer's Eve until the Spring Rain Day."

The room at Anna's Inn had been nice. A night's rest in a proper bed was rare. I was finished reminding him, and fixed him with a stern look instead.

"You have no sense of adventure," my brother told me. "I hope Keeper Edmund pays well this time."

Chapter VI

The aviary was a tall, sturdy granite block tower on the edge of one of the city's ancient inner walls. Many districts had grown from the feet of walls just like it. The Wrem Keep was long, a structure that was once a key point in one of the middle defensive rings to the city. There were other outer and inner walls with towers that hadn't fallen in the quake or were repaired since. The few who had the luxury of walking on the wind often marvelled at the view of Ankon City.

Whenever my brother or I took a moment to peer out of one of the narrow tower slits to catch sight of the view from there, it was a revelation. When we were afoot below, everything seemed larger than us, but from there everyone looked small, embraced by a city that had overgrown through the ages from the coastline to the distant farmlands. Opportunities to sightsee that day were rare, however. We couldn't afford to be caught idle.

We crawled into feces encrusted cages, nooks, and made nimble work of cleaning the roof with stiff brushes. "How do birds shit straight up?" my brother asked me as he was scraping matter off the inside of one of the roof hatches.

"Must have happened when the door was opened," I replied, having a chuckle.

"That door hasn't opened in my whole time here," said one of the tenders. He was a human twice our age, by my best estimation. "So, your friend there asks a good question."

How he earned the thankless task of scraping the floors clean, I never found out, but even over the cloth covering his nose and mouth I could see he was sour faced at the work.

I was thankful for one thing that day, aside from the meagre pay. They had moved all the pigeons to another aviary at the other end of the keep. We found old dead birds in a few of the cages, and another on the floor. Their corpses had dried to feather and bone, a testament to how badly kept the aviary was. Dust filled the air and stung our eyes as we scraped old bird dung off brick, metal, and wood. We wore rags over our noses and mouths, but I'll still never forget the taste that made it through that kerchief. It was chalky, with a strange sweet-bitter flavour that was difficult to dislodge.

"How's a little thievery looking now?" my brother asked in a low whisper as the day came to a close, and the aviary seemed as hot as an oven.

I didn't dignify his question with a response, but I can admit that I secretly saw his point. Neither of us were lazy people, shying from toil, but I remember fondly recalling the stress of pickpocketing and finding it preferable to the work in the aviary.

At the end of the day, we were each given four coppers and escorted through the servants corridors. When we emerged from the keep at the base of one of the ancient city walls, we were struck in the face by the thick fragrance of the city on the hot air. The sun had baked the bricks at our feet, and it still hung in the sky beaming its heat down on our heads. Just the same, that thick air was refreshing, and we were happy to be free for the late afternoon, even though we had been grossly underpaid. With the four coppers I had earned, I then had saved nine coppers, or nine one-hundredths of a silver lark. If we didn't stand apart from our own people, singled out as rebels against the King, we could have had better work, and made much more. Our pride wouldn't have it, though in retrospect I think we were foolish. The only crime we were known for was decrying the King's law in the Temple Square with several other rebel Ondi, all of them older. No fierce defiance had been recorded, or real crime committed at that point, but it wouldn't stay that way for long. I underestimated the depth of my brother's dissatisfaction with our lot, a mistake I regret to this day.

"Four coppers," he scoffed. "If that's pay for honest work, I can't imagine how miserable punishment must be."

We made haste to our next destination, the Temple Square, the second highest point in Ankon. After a long day on our knees, and an afternoon climbing around the precarious roof of that tower, the uphill walk through the busy streets wasn't welcome, but the reward that awaited us was enough to drive us on.

The city smelled cleaner as we climbed, and before long our scent – bird scat and sweat – began to draw a little attention. People would catch a whiff and look around, their gaze finally settling on us, two filthy little Ondi. We were thankful for it more often than not, as people took a hasty step away, giving us more room than we were accustomed to. You see, dried bird leavings and sweat make a paste with a particular odour, and I'll leave what that was like to your imaginations. My brother took more pleasure in parting the crowd than I did, but I admit to enjoying the show, as he smiled cordially at people as they regarded us with varying degrees of disgust.

"I wish the baths were open. There's no doubt where we've been once the scent strikes," I told him. "The smell's worse than expected, makes me wonder what they've been feeding those birds."

"It's work Lord Darlish won't force on his own servants, so who knows."

"I can certainly tell why. I don't think they'll let us in to the Piper tonight until we've had some time with a couple buckets."

"I have business before I wash this off," my brother told me quietly. "I want eggs tomorrow morning."

"You're not thinking of hitting the Thistledon coops?"

"In this state I'd be daft not to."

"Do I have to remind you that David Thistledon has hounds?"

"They'll be slow to respond while I reek of pigeon. You forget, he keeps his own messenger birds."

I couldn't help but smile at the thought and nod. "Sometimes you are smart enough to be family. Still, be ready to run. We can't afford a healer's touch for a dog bite."

He rolled his eyes, not offering a reply.

Our bellies were empty and rumbling their complaints at having nothing but traces of pigeon leavings coating their insides. We were glad to find even ground as we turned into the East Amblinton Square. The top of that grand hill was flattened into a square, with old buildings built from impossibly large blocks of stone. We joined a milling sea of people in front of the Mount Lamber Temple, our moods brightening.

The Shaper's Guildhall was the first sight offered by the Temple Square. It did its best to overtake the grandeur of the Temple with its lavishly decorated blue marble arches and a second storey fountain that crowned the entrance, but there was no besting the powerful view of the Mount Lamber Temple as one came around the corner.

The Temple was made of hardened glass and marble. My brother had looked closely at those glimmering pillars more than once and noticed the patterns left behind from when the craftspeople turned the sandstone to the hard, colourful glass it was. He couldn't read, but the lettering and detailed, colourful images that were left there over the ages were still impressive. When the entire continent of Brightwill quaked over a century before, leaving most ancient buildings damaged or completely broken, a few, like the Temple, had been preserved thanks to powerful warding spells maintained by the resident priests and magicians.

The columns rose four storeys high, holding heavy marble slabs aloft. The glimmering depictions along the thick walls held scenes ranging from the pious to the carnal. Innumerable tales were told there, all teaching a moral lesson or setting an example in the spaces between windows. There were eight storeys above ground and how deep the structure was remained a secret to all but a select few. It was a place of study and prayer for people of many faiths. More than that, it was a place for shrines.

Two grand chambers within, each with their own entrances at the left and right, were home to hundreds of shrines. The greatest of shrines were for royalty, others for great personalities, and still more were for people who had wealthy families. Some of the shrines rotted, the sponsors unable to afford the caretaker fee. Most of the little tables were maintained by family members and friends. A few of them were tended to by servants or guarded by family knights, and tributes were demanded by their households.

Regardless of how simple or ornate a shrine was, every one of them had several things in common. Each plot was granted by a priest, who measured it out by stretching one arm straight ahead, and another to his side: that determined how much space you were given. Unlucky or poor families would be assigned a very small priest for their measurements. The most important thing all the shrines had in common was their purpose. Those who believed in the malleability of life and death brought whatever offerings they could to the shrines built in honour of their loved ones because enough offerings, or the right offering, could bring that person back. The Planar Guides' word was expensive, but paying for advice from one on what to offer could mean the difference between randomly providing something that may not be of use to whoever was on the other side of that shrine and getting them across. Rumours of people returning from another plane after death were common, though sightings were rare. So rare, in fact, that we had only heard of an Ondi form our district witnessing a lady returning once in our lifetimes, and rumour had it that her family had given the Planar Guides the deed to their keep in the Midlands and sent Lady Lynnan an enchanted circlet.

We know now that Brightwill was one realm adrift in a universe of uncounted thousands. We've also learned the lessons that come with prying doors to those other places open, but in those days, the statue of Coriath stood in the middle of the largest shrine hall, his eyes closed and his arms open. It was a foolish notion, that you could bring loved ones back with baubles and prayers.

My brother and I avoided the overgrown chapels, but would sometimes venture into the main cathedral on the first floor. The foyer was adorned with tall statues honouring Deities both female and male, as well as animal and divine. It was the only Temple in which there was no preaching, only altar offerings for deities, quiet prayer, and the meeting of various heads of religion and state. This was a place for the older gods, the ones most people believed in before Coriath came and began teaching thousands of humans in the ways of magic. It was the only place where you couldn't find scars from the War, and Hyra Ondi stood between her wolves with a crown of flowers in her hair. I didn't really believe in our Goddess, but I admired that old wood carving, probably because it seemed to beckon to a time when we knew the way back to the great woodlands, where our people lived in nature. No one needed coin to eat, or permission to make their bed in the forest, and the minds of animals weren't clouded by the concerns that plagued them in cities. I had romantic notions of the forest back then, but young people should have such overgrown fantasies. None of that prepared me for the reality of wilderness when I found myself confronted by it some time later, but that's another story.

In those days, bread was distributed to any who came to the Temple once a day. The Shaper's Guild was in charge of it back then, and I recall the bread being particularly good. Perhaps it was because there were so many lords competing for attention during that time, or because I was hungrier, I'll never know for certain. The Shaper's Guild and the lords had an arrangement in place where the lords would donate bread to the Temple and the Shaper's Guild. The amount and quality of the bread determined how much time they could have with the Shaper's Guild Heralds, who would announce weddings, executions, publicize disgraces, give eulogies, decry the acts of criminals, give decrees, and share other news from that lord. We didn't honestly care about all that upper city politicking; we let the guild herald go on while we feasted on rich bread.

We took our place in line that day like most others. I spent my time reading the stories on the nearest pillar, and can't recall which I was reading that day, maybe Tuss and the Charger – known now as the tale of the Dwarf and the Steed. You know it, the one where Tuss Ninth Finger tries to tame a horse four times the proper size for his height only to realize it's his ancestor returned to teach him a lesson about patience.

40

My brother didn't really know how to read well - letters tested his patience - so he watched the crowd.

Carts piled high with bread emerged from between the temple pillars. Where they kept them until it was time to distribute the dinner bread was a mystery to us then, but the fact that there was usually enough for those who arrived before sunset was all we really cared about. There was always a stir at the front of the crowd when the bread came into view, and the keepers always managed to calm the people.

Despite our mistrust of most priests, we were thankful that the Temple was different. Before long the group sorted into lines as the priests, priestesses, and various magical practitioners - teachers and students alike - passed out loaf after loaf. One magician, a man called Chonolo, somehow made three copies of himself and made a great show of being in more than one place at once. "An illusion?" my brother asked quietly.

I watched the four of them for a long moment then slowly shook my head. "Not one like I've ever seen. The doppelgangers are perfect copies of the original, from what I can tell, yet they're all doing different things. It's like he copied himself, really copied himself. It's as if Chonolo has three brothers."

"How do you know he doesn't?"

I turned towards my brother with a 'tsk' and shook my head. "Everyone knows Chonolo. He was named the Master Wizard here just last year and served in the Void War."

"I don't keep up on Temple politics." He shrugged.

"You were here at his celebration feast."

"I've been here for every feast," he said dismissively.

"You remember the feast where they brought out entire hogs on spits?"

"Oh! The pork! That feast was for him? Remind me to thank him if I'm ever in shouting distance."

"Sometimes I forget your memories rest in your stomach."

"Does anything else really matter? So, which Chonolo is the real one?"

I nodded towards my best guess and made direct eye contact with the dark haired human wizard, sending a mild mental acknowledgement in his direction.

A grin spread the man's black beard apart as he nodded at me. The smile faded as that kindly gaze took in the state of my filthy, tattered clothing.

"Think you've been spotted," my brother chuckled. "How'd you know that was the real one, anyway?"

"I don't know, just a feeling. It's only a trick, after all. If I were better at seeing the pattern of living things I could probably describe it in writing so someone could try it."

"Some trick. I'd like to be in more than one place at once. Easy alibi."

The Shaper's Guild Herald was getting ready to speak. He was a large man with more chins and glimmering rings than anyone could count at a glance and he mounted a tall pillar, as if he needed its help to draw attention to himself. I couldn't help but look him up and down as he paused a moment to catch his breath from the short climb. His boots were made of soft leather embellished with blue silk to match his thin cloak. He very nearly spilled out of a long white silken coat, obviously made for him when he was somewhat thinner.

His chest was adorned with three gaudy broaches. One had a bell in its centre, marking him as a crier. The next featured a green fox, and the final one beside it featured a shield and three stars, detailing the two great houses he was pledged to. One was House Crevan, that of Brightwill's Western King, while the other was House Soletra, a great house that had married into the upper echelon of the local royal family. Which one this crier was born into was anyone's guess.

"Hail one, hail all! It is my honour to make the matters and decrees of the kingdom known!" boomed the man, whose voice carried over the crowd like an intrusive wave. "King Hosten has decreed that it is a criminal act to perish or be otherwise slain in his court. Spirit catchers will be in attendance to ensure this law is upheld. Lord Marros, Patron of House Arimosa has recovered and is in good health, to the delight of his heirs. The marriage of his granddaughter, Lady Elina, to Lord Barl is to take place on the third day of Flourishing." The overgrown human took a deep breath and mopped the sweat from his brow with a pristine, embroidered cloth. "Lady Tisira, Matron of House Kimorian, is announcing the forced withdrawal of her first born son, Dyle, from a challenge at melee issued by Surpo of House Wain."

This announcement was greeted with a wave of laughter and jeers from the multitude that had gathered. "No sport from him while he's at his mother's teat!" cried someone well behind us.

We laughed aloud at the jeer. Everyone knew Dyle was a grown man. A pretty, tall, fair-haired man who was seen as a dandy thanks to his overprotective mother. Lady Tisira had a different reputation, however. She was fierce and unyielding, as cold as her cool complexion and as sharp as her thin features. What was worse, she was known as a steadfast ally to King Hosten. The public announcement of her son's withdrawal was as important as the announcement of the challenge days before. The date had been set for an open arena exposition that would come the very next day, and with one fewer event, excitement for the spectacle was beginning to wilt. It would be the last such event until early summer, which was months away.

The crier went on, pretending not to hear the jeers and laughter of the crowd. The affairs of the King and lords who could afford the cost of public announcements were more an entertainment than something that affected our daily lives.

The Dwarven sorceress, a young woman in a green and brown light robe and a blush on her cheeks, chose a thick round loaf for each of us, and unlike everyone we'd stood near or strode past that day, she didn't turn her nose or gaze away when we came near. "How are you two?"

I didn't recognize her, but I thought she may have met my brother sometime, perhaps at one of the taverns where he enjoyed dicing. Regardless, I replied as though I'd known her for years. "We reek of honest work, but the day has been kind," I told her.

"If you remain here, I could show you to the Temple basins inside, I don't think anyone would mind, considering the legacy of your master," she whispered. Then I remembered where I knew her from; she was an acquaintance of my Master, Nauso, who was imparting some Ondi-Ne magic to a few dwarven students in secret. Dwarves were Ondi as well, the tallest and thickest of our kind, the Ondi-Un. I often considered them the natural intermediaries between us and the humans. Her name was Uwren Felltree, and she was one of the brighter ones, with an independent streak I'd learn about in the days to come.

Just then a clamour arose to our left as an armoured man atop a tall horse and his fellows were pressing through the masses. Their heads were held high, their shining armour gleamed as they pressed towards the front of the temple. "Bread and wine for me and my men! We begin a turn on guard for the King!" demanded the leader.

Uwren tried to get my brother's attention back to the matter at hand, touching his hand with a grand loaf of bread, but he took it without looking. "Thank you, priestess," he said, not tearing his eyes away from the cause of the commotion.

"She's a sorceress," I corrected.

"Sorceress, thank you, *sorceress*," he corrected through a half-mouthful of bread. As he chewed through a generous piece of the thick, nutty, cheesy bread, he followed me to the side so we weren't in the way of the moving line, without altering his gaze. "That armour he's wearing, his horse, it's worth a row of houses in Highkeep."

I looked closely for the first time, barely able to see between a crowd of humans that were getting ready to sit on the Temple stair. The etchings on his armour were symbols of protection; he was dressed to kill magical practitioners, hunt down mad spirits, or something more dire. He was the sort of man they sent after our kind during the War.

I looked away. "Eat your bread," I told my brother then. I took a generous bite, trying to press the mental image of my executed parents out of my mind. I knew how they were killed, I'd overheard it a few days before celebrating my tenth year. Our parents fought until they knew we were safe, killing no human, but drawing them away from the Woodland District, which was in a different part of the city then, a better part. They were captured. They were brought before the King and then they were drowned in a vat at his feet.

The knight that had my brother's attention was ready to hunt Ondi-Ne, and Ava-Ondi. People who were learning the ways of magic even though it was forbidden for them.

I didn't care about the transgressions some of my people made against the humans before I was born. I knew my parents weren't members of the ruling class, they had nothing to do with suppressing humans. All I knew was that there was a dangerous hunter nearby, and he'd kill me just as soldiers like him drowned my parents. I elbowed my brother, and went on chewing my bread.

"Clear a path, I say!" bellowed the knight. The crowd fell silent as the priests froze. The knights had no authority there. In fact, it was custom for them to approach the temple as penitents, to request the blessing of a priest. It was normally done well before or after the passing of the bread.

One of Chonolo's copies took one of the smaller loaves from a cart then dipped a chipped ceramic cup into a bucket and presented it to the lead knight. "I have no wine for you, but the bread is next to divine," the bearded fellow announced joyously. "Come, everyone! Tonight, we dine with the King's own knights!"

The knight batted the cup from Chonolo's hand, sending it into the crowd. "I won't drink that brack!"

A collective gasp of shock spread throughout the crowd. Everyone was watching the great Wizard Chonolo and the knight, even the herald, who had just finished his announcements and would have normally retreated to the Shaper's Guildhall.

"Back of the line, you bloody twat," grumbled my brother. I think he only realized he'd said it aloud when everyone around him, myself included, turned to stare at him in shock.

"Who said that?" roared the knight, raising his visor so he could better look across the multitude. He was a clean shaven man with piercing blue eyes and a square jaw. He looked down his nose at the crowd around him, glancing this way and that for the insulting culprit.

I could see my brother's face turning red. His temper got the better of him, and he mounted the temple steps. I tried to catch the back of his tunic, but missed. "Don't you do anything I'll regret," I whispered to him urgently.

"Sorry, brother. If I don't take credit, he'll just punish some other poor sod." He turned his attention to the knight, whistled shrilly and shouted, "Here!"

The knight looked around, aimlessly, glowering at the crowd in general. Everyone else heard the whistle, most knew where it came from and some even pointed. Their advice went unheard, as though the knight simply wouldn't acknowledge them. I was terrified, and told my brother, "get down or I'll never forgive you!" in the harshest whisper I could manage. It wasn't too late, the knight was still oblivious to the little Ondi-Ne standing above the bread line at the top of the Temple stair, but my brother wouldn't be ignored. He sighed, then climbed atop an empty cart as he tore off a nutty chunk of his bread.

"Don't even think-" I began to warn him.

"Oi! I'm over here you dandy cunt!" he shouted as he hurled his bread so hard he nearly unbalanced himself. If the crowd was in shock before, they were astounded then, as the missile struck the side of the knight's helmet with a 'ping' sound that echoed across the square.

The knight's cold blue eyes turned to his assailant. Only too late my brother decided that what he was doing was unwise. He shifted one of his feet off the cart into the open air so he could make a quick escape.

"Seize him! He has assaulted one of the King's men! Doing so is the same as assailing the King himself!" The knights behind him were beginning to move, slowly, more conscious of the crowd around their horses than their leader.

"Good! I hope they march me straight into Gregor Hall so I can tell him all about how his poncey highborn knight was taking food from the luckless!" My brother's voice was shrill, cracked with fear, but seeing that the crowd wasn't parting for the knights gave him the little courage he needed to feel more outraged than fearful. The crowd wasn't dispersing, or parting, or helping. They were dumbstruck, or amused, but definitely not moving out of the way.

I don't know why, but that prompted my brother to throw something else at the offended knight. He threw it so hard it looked as though his arm would leave its socket. It wasn't until it glanced off the top of the horse's heavily armoured head and struck the knight on the chin that I realized that my brother had thrown his blunted chisel instead of bread.

I watched in disbelief as the giant knight was unbalanced. With a great shuffle and crash, the man fell from his horse.

"Run!" I told my brother as an arrow struck the cart he was standing on.

In a heartbeat he was off the cart and turned around. My heart sank as several city guards rushed to the cart, drawing swords.

"Hold! Hold your arms!" boomed Chonolo. "Honour can be satisfied without endangering the innocent."

The knight had managed to regain his footing and was being helped onto his horse by his squire. "Ondi have no honour! He's a dog! Cut him down!"

The soldiers weren't listening, thankfully, but didn't sheathe their swords, either.

"I will sponsor this boy in the tournament if you will fight him, Sir Grelor!" the Wizard Chonolo announced.

"Fight him? I'd sooner fight the Zutari Hordes than sully my sword with his foul blood!"

I didn't know what my brother was thinking, but with an empty hand, he pretended he was about to toss another stone at the knight.

Sir Grelor flinched so hard he almost fell from his horse before fully mounting.

"This mongrel's got you shaking in your plates!" my brother jeered. The crowd laughed, only making the situation worse.

I was barely aware of it, but I'd climbed the temple stair myself and was only a few feet from the cart where my brother stood. "Don't look behind you," I told him just loudly enough so he could hear.

Of course that was more of an invitation than he could stand resisting, so my brother looked over his shoulder. The soldiers were still standing ready, watching as though they expected my brother to leap off the cart and scurry away any moment.

My brother returned his gaze to Sir Grelor in time to start a staring contest with the knight. "You couldn't best me, Sir, not in a fair fight! Give me my match and I'll show all these people how one takes a brash simpleton down." It was a kind of madness! A grin spread across his face, my brother looked eager! Actually eager! "Again! I'll show them again!" he corrected.

I cleared my throat and muttered, "Laying it on a little thick, aren't we?"

One of Chonolo's doppelgangers, reduced to my size, appeared behind me and pulled me down the stairs. "It's too late, you can't help him if you get implicated."

I reluctantly backed down the stairs with the doppelganger of the great wizard, who had taken up my brother's cause for reasons that escaped me at the time.

"I'll give you your match, High Wizard, but not because he goads. I'll give it to you on the condition that this rat's head will be mounted on a pike in this square and no one will get any bread until the crows have picked it clean!"

My heart sank, the crowd erupted, and I found myself suddenly ashamed.

"I'll allow his head to be put up, but the people will have their bread," the Chonolo closest to the knight bargained.

"Done! My guardsmen will carry him to an arena cell, where he'll wait to be cut down."

"No bargain!" my brother shouted as the guards started from the street to the temple stair. "I can get there on my own! Or maybe priests could escort me?" His objection fell on deaf ears. Of course he wanted to escape, and it would be easier to do so if they sent the wrong priests or sorcerers to watch over him, but his greater concern must have been the beating he could expect from the guards, or from the knights the moment he was out of common sight.

"Hush, Chonolo will see that no harm comes to you," Uwren the Sorceress reassured him.

"You're such an idiot!" I shouted at him. Somewhere between concern and shock was a deep well of anger and frustration. "You just do whatever pops into your thick head!"

"A little sympathy for the condemned?" my brother asked, fixing me with a smile as though he was just teasing me like he used to when we were younger. I could see through it; he was terrified.

"Maybe you can just run in circles around the arena until he dies of exhaustion!" I was angrier than he was frightened.

"Oh, you draw from a deep well of sympathy, you do." The guards were carefully surrounding him, expecting him to slip between them. Any one of them was at least three times his weight and twice his height. "All right, in the absence of family, I find this world cold. Take me to my prison," he said melodramatically as he offered his wrists for shackles.

"Leave it to you to make a farce of this," I spat. "What am I going to do without you?"

Chapter VII

While Naze told his brother's tale, the aisles of the small lecture hall filled until there was absolutely no room left. Doril was at his side, and he recognized that his master needed a break. "Please file out if you would," Doril said. "Quietly and carefully."

"We'll reconvene shortly in the main auditorium," Naze said. "I only need a moment." The memory of his brother being taken by the guards had returned with greater clarity than Naze could have predicted.

"Are you sure?" Doril asked in a whisper.

"I'm going to finish telling this story. The next part must be seen, not just orated."

"You're going to conjure the past using light?"

"In light and shadow, yes, I'll have to retrieve something from my rooms first," Naze replied. "But yes, if the truth is going to come out, then it should be witnessed as purely as possible."

"I can send someone to get whatever it is you need," Doril offered.

"No, I'll be the only one who can find this, go on and get the lecture hall ready."

"Yes, Master," Doril said.

"Do you think any of them have guessed at my brother's identity?" Naze asked. Watching the students depart, he could see some of them looked more concerned than thrilled.

"In a word: yes," Doril replied. "You may as well identify him soon. If the next part of the story takes us where I think it will, then there's no point in hiding it any longer."

"I didn't give our students enough credit. I thought I'd be able to tell more of the story, earn more sympathy for him with the truth before I had to name him."

"The pitfall of a well-educated student body," Doril said. "Sometimes they get ahead of you."

Naze allowed himself to be led out to the hallway and made his way back to his rooms using secret passages. He knew a few of his students saw him turn towards a wall and disappear into the stone, but it didn't bother him in the slightest. Those pupils would try it themselves and fail; the walls knew who could pass and who had to go the long way.

Once he reached his apartment, he made haste to his observatory tower. It was only two extra turns on a spiral stairway from his sitting room, then two steps back at the very top, and he reappeared in a large cavern beneath the Isle of Wilders. The transition between the two places was so seamless that it still took his mind a moment to adjust to the notion that he was months away from his previous location by land and sea.

The cavern was lit with blue amber blood, a fluid that was magic itself, and produced a ghostly light in small concentrations. The lamps of the Cinder Cave were filled with the stuff, and they illuminated the space with the illusion of a starry sky. Three silver moons shed enough white light for Naze to see clearly in all directions.

Stone paths led across the water inside the cave to different dry sections. To his left there were two libraries. Books, scrolls, and telling eyes gathered by him and secret cohorts were caged there. To his right were two paths that led to the vaults, where artefacts, riches, and mementos were stored at one end. At the other end of the vaults were dangerous articles. Behind him was the path he took least, the one that led to the cells. They built five, but only used one. Charthanga, the founder of the Cinder Men, still laboured against his chains and tried to speak, even though they took his lower jaw away so he could never conjure with words again. He would have his immortality, but as a powerless prisoner. Naze could feel the malicious wizard's will, just at the edge of his consciousness, trying to feel his way past the barriers he'd erected around his mind and spirit.

Naze took a moment to block the Cinder Master completely, then drew in the healing power of the water at his feet. He could feel the innocent aquatic life there, a perfect cycle of nature underway. He'd passed the lesson that life was sympathetic on to his students more times than he could count. By being amongst the living and close to nature, one could become a part of that life. Just by being in that cave, where there was an ocean cavern at his feet filled with energy, he could direct his body to be reinvigorated. It cost the wildlife around him nothing, because, when at peace, living things prefer to heal rather than wither.

Even at his advanced age, the pools were soothing and invigorating. The ache in his knee was gone after a moment, and the cool air of the cavern nearly made him forget the heat of the Amber Refuge.

The presence of Charthanga was blocked; his hate could remain in the confinement of his iron cell. With the malevolent noise gone, Naze could feel the presence of an old friend approaching. He was bearing an object of incredible power, the only one in Brightwill, perhaps the only one of its kind. The Enduring Light, fixed into a new form.

Naze was relieved that he wouldn't have to walk ahead through the cave system to get to the island village of Usho. He opened his eyes in time to see Oroza slip from the water to the stone path. His long clawed feet made easy purchase on the ground, and he stood upright. The dragon had grown over the decades, true, but not as much as he should have. The humans did eventually get their hands on him and use their quick amber to fuse his wings together so he would never fly. They hung against his back, out of the way.

Scars from misadventures and imprisonment marked his grey-blue body so deeply that some scales would not regrow after moulting. His right eye was lifeless thanks to the final battle against Charthanga. He'd sustained other dire injuries during the end of the Cinder War; the small dragon was still recovering, but recovering well. His right forearm regenerated, even his broken teeth were falling out so new ones could grow in, but that eye would never see again. The dragon was only half a head taller than Naze, small for a creature his age. "We grow lazy with old age," Naze said with a smile. "I was just thinking on how relieved I was that I wouldn't have to find you in the village."

"You may be growing lazy, but I fly underwater," Oroza said with an impish smile. "The humans didn't get my tail." He whipped his long tail across a pool, splashing Naze a little.

He wiped the water from his cheek and nodded. "True enough."

"Happy birthday," Oroza said, offering a bauble that was prettier than Naze expected. Six rings were fused together to form a sphere, made of white gold, and a smaller, platinum ring spun silently in the centre. The dragon was a masterful craftsman. "I assume the great work is ongoing?"

"Yes, absolutely. I'm more sure that this is the right thing to do as the day goes on."

"A spell in the form of a story. Is it comforting to return to the ways of your ancestors?"

"It's easier than I expected, but I can feel the momentum of it all, the story, the power, the living and the dead crying out for healing now that they know the world can be mended," Naze replied. "I'm afraid the telling of this story has already given me a tendency towards melodrama."

Oroza laughed, his older arm stroking the forearm of his freshly regenerated one. "Good, this should be a telling for the ages. The beginning has been enjoyable, but I'll admit that I'm looking forward to your illusions, to seeing Riv again. He was an exciting creature."

"You've been listening from here? From the other side of the world?" Naze asked. "Have you really become so powerful?"

"Only through meeting the demands of the Cinder War," Oroza replied. "It's not the kind of power I ever wanted, but I'm learning to bend it to my will, enough so I can hear and see you as I while the time away. How is your resolve, now that you've conjured memories of your brother?"

"Firmer than ever. This examination of conscience is exactly what I needed," Naze replied.

"Good. Make sure you tell them about his zeal, even during Riv's questionable acts," Oroza told him. "It was what I admired most about him."

"I will," Naze said. "You can be sure I will."

"Charthanga knows something is happening, he's listening to everything that goes on in these caves. He knows your masterwork is at hand, and wants nothing more than to bend it to his own ends. I've made sure he can't interfere."

"Thank you, I couldn't have had a better friend over the years," Naze.

"Now, we both know that's not true, but I'll take the compliment regardless. You've become a master, whether you desired it or not. Your search for knowledge has resulted in power, and I look forward to your rising even higher this evening. Until then, regale us with your remembrances. Riv will live again through you, as he should."

Chapter VIII

By the time Naze arrived at the podium in the main lecture hall, Doril was almost finished summarizing the story he told earlier that morning. The audience stirred at his arrival, but kept listening to Doril for the most part.

The main feature of the hall was a high main dais, with four benches set in a semi-circle around a podium. Naze quietly finished emerging from the curtain hiding a modest back sitting room for speakers, and sat on the dais.

Doril glanced at him and Naze smiled, resting his elbow on a crossed leg, and his chin on his hand, exaggerating a posture of rapt attention. The audience, nearly two thousand in number, chuckled at the rare antic for a moment before Doril shook his head and continued.

Naze relaxed and looked out at the auditorium. The main seating extended out and up from the bottom of the speaker's dais, in a half-circle. The rearmost and longest row was several stages up from the level of the dais. Above the main seating were three balconies; each had three stages of seating, and only the top one was empty. He couldn't help think that the auditorium would never be full during his tenure, there just weren't enough Ondi and people from friendly races left in Brightwill.

The white marble and oak auditorium was a work of art, however, and he had many fond recollections of attending plays, lectures from peers, and even a few interesting student presentations. Scanning the crowd, he could see that his storytelling had drawn the instructors and mentors along with their students. They tended the younger groups like shepherds, and policed the older crowd like wardens. Most of the instructors had a deep respect for him, and seeing that nearly all of them were in attendance was a welcome sight to Naze.

Lizabe was there in her wide brimmed white and blue hat. Looking down from where Naze sat, he couldn't see anything but the top of that hat; it was so wide, and she was so small. She was the shortest Ondi he'd ever seen, and had a sweet, high voice, but she carried a thin wicker staff that was taller than any of the other instructors, and her voice could reach shrill heights. That, along with a sharp intelligence, impressive memory, and wicked wit made her the prime instructor for some of the most promising adolescent students. To her credit, she rarely had to raise her voice, and she almost never poked a wayward student with her staff. She stood out as one of the greatest weavers of reality, as far as Naze was concerned. He'd seen her win duels simply by changing the effects of another magician's efforts; starting a spell on her own was rarely something she had to do to win an engagement. She was instrumental in mending the tears Charthanga opened in their reality to invite a strange breed of dragons in. They were creatures who turned city and woodland alike into raging inferno fields, and made their beds in red hot glass. They were not the beings that once graced the skies of Brightwill a century before, and even with the rifts to their plane closed, they would never be entirely eradicated. Even so, if it weren't for Lizabe's talents, those doorways would still be open, and Brightwill would be entirely lost.

Her husband was at her side. Although he was shorter than the average Ondi, he was nowhere near as miniature as Lizabe, but he was widely built and muscled, though you could barely tell through his long black beard. The glorious chin growth hung below his knees, and made him look grizzled on long days. Regardless of all that, Kovak almost always looked friendly; a glance into his eyes told most people he had a light heart. No one would ever suspect that he was the dominant master of the Way and kinetic magic, a sort of fighting art involving a lot of forms Naze didn't practice enough. He bragged that no student had singed or so much as touched his beard during lessons since he started, and it was true, no one could match Kovak the Great. The only mystery Naze couldn't solve about the man was how he became so agile while growing up underground with the Ondi-Un, or Dwarves, as they were sometimes called. He was Lizabe's defender throughout the Cinder War, keeping physical threats away from her while she wielded a different sort of power. Neither of them celebrated war, but they served as comrades to Naze in three, seeing the good that he wanted to do. When it came time to build the refuge atop the remains of the great temple, they were at his side as well, looking forward to brighter days. He desperately wished he could give them that.

As though realizing they were being noticed, the pair passed the responsibilities of watching their students to their most senior acolytes and climbed the side of the dais. Lizabe took the first few steps, struggling a little, then levitated the rest of the way, keeping pace with her husband, who held the end of his beard in one hand as he ascended to the dais.

They were no more than two years younger than Naze, but the pair still looked more spry and youthful than he. He could only imagine that their secret lay in their long, happy companionship. Lizabe embraced him briefly. "I'm so thrilled that you're talking about Riv today, we both are," she told him in a low whisper. "I knew your masterwork would come through story, but I would never have guessed it would have been his."

"He deserves to have his side told," Kovak said as he patted Naze's shoulder with a broad hand. "I didn't know him long, but it didn't take long for me to grow a fondness."

It was then that Naze realized that Kovak had met Riv. For all the detail he remembered about those days, he'd completely forgotten that.

"He forgot you met him," Lizabe said as she hopped up onto the bench to Naze's left.

Kovak joined her. "Well, shame on him," he replied, chuckling quietly.

"I apologize," Naze said, running his hand through his short grey hair. "So much happened back then."

"I wish I was there. I wonder if you'll have time to retell our meeting?" Lizabe asked.

"I don't think so, I'm sorry," Naze said. "Though that would be one they'd remember."

Kovak chuckled. "Aye, it would. I hope to enjoy it again someday soon."

"I'm sure you will," Naze replied.

"Times worth remembering," Lizabe said. "I remember the years we wandered after Riv. We had so much fun, saw so much."

"I remember almost starving in the Narwood. My stomach has a sharper memory than my mind, I think," Kovak said apologetically to his wife.

"Too many blows to the head," Lizabe replied. "Love ya just the same."

Doril finished telling his summary of the morning's tale, and looked to Naze, who took a breath and nodded. "There are lessons in what you'll hear, so listen well," Doril told the gathered masses. His voice was carried to them through an enchantment in the podium so they could all hear. "To regale you with tales from his youth, I present the holder of the Amber Seat, Master Naze Kinu."

"Good luck," Lizabe said as Naze stood and took the podium. He found the applause at the act annoying. He didn't know why, but there it was. Doril took his place on the bench behind him.

"Silence, I beg of you," Naze said with a smile that was a little forced. "I think we should all take a moment to close our eyes, clear our minds, and take in the sensations of this time and this place before I begin."

He was the first to close his eyes and open his mind. His consciousness drifted briefly, and he found himself looking over the ruin of Brightwill Radial, the very centre of the old city. Where stone towers, rows of houses, arching bridges with entire villages built on them once stood strong, there were ruins. A crack in the ground miles deep marked the centre. A jungle of trees, vines, and other growth reached up and outward from that crevasse. For miles in each direction the city was overgrown, a result of the last moments of the Cinder War. His school was built on the nearest mountain top, overlooking the ruins.

Beyond the horizon, where Brightwill continued on out of sight, matters only grew worse. There were Kings who maintained strongholds, bands of roving raiders, nomadic groups scurrying from one ruin to another, burned towns, ashen forests, and blackened rivers. Naze knew every stronghold, every standing city, and his school was where most of their master wizards were trained over the last generation. Without the Amber Refuge, most of those other rare, safe places would have fallen long ago. Even though he played a critical role in keeping people alive in Brightwill, he was saddened. The Amber Refuge was never built to train wizards for war, but it had become its primary purpose. It would not do.

It only took Naze a moment to return his attention to the podium and the present. The auditorium was silent except for the faint sound of beating hearts, breathing people, and a muffled cough. He began speaking before everyone finished observing the still moment. "A few of you have begun to puzzle out who my brother was. He was a more notorious man than myself, and that's saying something. Riv Kinu was the only blood relation I had left in the world when I was in my late formative years. He was someone I criticized and admired at the same time, only I didn't realize that I actually admired him until he had been gone for years."

A few of his student body, even some of the instructors, regarded him dubiously. Most of the people gathered seemed eager to hear more, however, so he pressed on before any of the people who disliked Riv's reputation could interrupt.

Chapter IX

"Riv was a man of the moment. Whatever place he found himself in, or activity he was about, he was focused on that and only that. In the years of his absence I've had time to reflect on his ability to only regard his world one heart beat at a time, and found that one can lead a rich life when you're making the most of every single moment. He disliked resting, but slept like the dead. His patience for discussion was short, but he kept the best company he could find. His acts were often reckless, but I've never seen anyone more apt at manoeuvring through troubled times.

"Unfortunately, his recklessness outdid his cunning when he insulted an important knight, eventually knocking the puffed-up King's man from his saddle. While Riv was brought to the stocks, I was held to have a conversation with the Great Chonolo himself, in a chamber beneath Mount Lamber Temple, the very one that once stood less than two hundred feet from where we are now. He offered condolences, and told me, 'I can sponsor your brother, but that is all. He will have to duel that knight on terms determined by his lords. I'm sorry, I have only bought him a night to live. On the brighter side, my servants and the temple guards have begun ushering your people into a private garden on the top of the temple. They came for second announcements, as always, and I didn't want any of them to suffer from any bullying. I can have you escorted there once we're finished here. I wish I could do more, but the will of the kingdom itself motivates the continued suppression of your people. Your district will have to be moved again, most likely, and I don't know where this King, or his Prince will put you.'"

"We are not suppressed," interrupted a woman. Her voice sounded high and reedy, like an Ava-Ondi, but she had a strange accent. My instincts sent me to my knees as she came around the corner. She was only half a hand taller than me, but her narrow features and dainty physique made her seem much more. She was one of the overthrown ones, Ava-Ondi, former rulers of all the Brightwill Kingdoms before the Great War. "Stand, our people don't sit on thrones, if they did I would have been executed long ago."

"She wore garb that was once typical of her people, and immodestly, I might add. Her robes were reduced to two long cloth panels, one flowing down the front, the other in the back, tied together with several silver chains. My head didn't spin at the sight of her ensemble - I have to admit that I found her bird-like and unattractive - but I was staggered by the realization that I could only be standing in the presence of Rakiz, the Betrayer.

"When the highest Aza-Ondi royal family members were making good their escape, it was Rakiz who made sure that Coriath's greatest disciples were standing in front of the portal site, and they were slaughtered. Legend said she strangled the last in line to take the Vanod Throne to death herself, the great grandson of her Queen, a toddler, and that is how she demonstrated her loyalty to the new Kings of Brightwill.

"I'll spare you the research, and tell you that I would discover that the rumours were true. She was instrumental in destroying the royal lines that ruled over Brightwill for centuries. I was on my knees because of what my mentor at the time taught me about her, that she was a sorceress of unparalleled skill, with forbidden knowledge and a wealth of secrets. If there was a master of rarefied Ava-Ondi magic, she was the one, but few practitioners enjoyed that fact.

"I immediately disliked her. Tiny jewels were woven into her black hair with silver thread, and her blue garb was made of fine light silk. Her fingers, even her toes, were dressed in rings. "All Ondi are free, and we will find our place amongst the new rulers," she said, her gaze settling on me. I rose from my knees slowly, feeling like I could drown in her ghostly blue eyes. "The power begins with people like you, Naze of the Ondi-Ne, the gifted have a right to rule."

"High Sorceress Rakiz," Chonolo said, "Forgive me for not presenting you, someone of your stature should not enter a room without proper announcement."

"No apology is necessary, the influence of my presence alone is announcement enough. You may go, priest," Rakiz told him without sparing him a glance.

With that, Chonolo and everyone else in the room left swiftly, wordlessly. "I have foreseen a terrible destiny for your brother, I'm sorry."

I was stunned. A sorceress who navigated through the most dangerous war for our people was telling me she foresaw the worst fate for my brother, my last living relative. I finally scraped a few words from my dry throat. "I don't know what to do, High Sorceress."

"Please, call me 'Mistress,'" she told me. Her tone remained formal, as though she were speaking to me from a throne. "I am in Ankon looking for a fresh pupil, and you are a prime candidate. Your potential is so muted that it took that incident at the temple with your brother for me to see you. A new destiny is already dawning for me even as I speak to you, as you are being brought to the moment when you make a decision."

I admit to being brash, as most youthful people are, and in my brashness, I didn't immediately see what anything she was saying had to do with my brother's predicament. My impatience was growing so quickly that I was short with her. "The only destiny I care about right now is my brother's, and if you're not going to help, I'm going to have to find someone who will."

"Your brother carries your heart more than any being in this world," she told me sympathetically. "I propose a trade. If you become my student, and study here, in the temple for one year, I will save your brother's life tomorrow. I can not guarantee that he will come away from the arena with no injuries at all, but he will survive if I intervene at the right moment."

In that moment I saw no other way to save him. My master was handling the relocation of our people, if what Chonolo was saying was true, and even if he wasn't, he'd have his hands full. Anything Riv did in the arena would cause a backlash against our people; it was the way of things then, and we were so few. Any lord or lady in the realm could command our eradication, and we would be lost before any friends we had, Ondi-Un, human, or any other, could come to our aid. I truly believed that my master would have to keep the larger picture in mind, that my brother had brought us to such a situation that we were truly alone, and that Rakiz was offering the easiest way out.

The promise she made wouldn't mean much coming from anyone else, but she was known to be powerful politically as well as magically. I could only agree, even though I felt I was betraying my good master, Nauso, and all my people, but I was desperate in my seemingly solitary situation. "When can you save him?"

"The moment will come tomorrow," she replied.

"You'll be able to keep him out of the arena?" I asked.

"I can't, no one outside of high royalty can now. He'll fight the third Prince of King Jonne, that is inevitable. The outcome is something I may be able to manipulate."

"You can guarantee nothing, then?"

"If I fail to save him, you will be free. If I do save him, you will be my pupil for a year."

"Save him, and I'll go with you."

I was immediately sent to the Acolytes' Dormitory, and I was not allowed to see any of my people. I felt isolated, unnerved, and slept fitfully. The stone walls seemed to release all the heat from the day through the night, and I couldn't stop thinking about what was being done to my brother that evening while I slept in a soft bed.

Chapter X

Little did I know, that the knight Riv insulted and embarrassed, Sir Grelor, was making an appearance in the dungeons of King Hosten. The efforts to take down the artefacts and carvings of the previous regime failed in that place. Inscriptions made to keep the prisoners awake, to keep them a breath away from comfort at all times were still where the ruling Ava-Ondi put them. Those same inscriptions in brick would keep some humans on edge during their visits, and if that didn't accomplish the old rulers' goals, the markings made by machines that once tortured their kind – a set of divots in a wall, mounting formations in the brick, or blood stains that ran so deep that they couldn't be scrubbed – would accomplish the same goal.

Riv told me that in the quiet moments before Sir Grelor arrived, he swore he sensed a chorus of screams just at the edge of his hearing. I have been to those dungeons since, I listened for the screams, and without conjuring, I found the magic the Ava-Ondi left behind to make a record of all the beings they tortured in their dungeons. Prisoners truly did hear what they claimed to in that dungeon for a long while after the humans took residence.

The guards who dragged Riv from his bed of straw were short, surprisingly short for humans. "Are you part Dwarf?" Riv asked one of them whose hair had grown down over his eyes. "Great people, Dwarves, Ondi-Un, we call them. I've got some Dwarf on my mother's side, they say that's where I get my heavy brow," he rattled on as they carried him down the dungeon hall so his feet barely brushed the ground.

"No," said the human.

"Well, one of you must be, otherwise, how are you so short?" Riv took a moment to rephrase as one of the guards sneered. "I mean, so well suited to your obviously gainful employment, the job security down here must be assured, most humans couldn't walk down here, since they're gifted with such great…" they rounded the corner into the main chamber, where the ceiling was tall enough to permit Sir Grelor. "…height," Riv finished as the seven foot tall knight grinned his gleaming white teeth at him. Those teeth would be a focal point for my brother when he told people about Grelor, I don't know why, but there you have it.

"Little boy," Grelor said, flexing a long varnished switch. "It's time I taught you some manners."

"Trying to skip the fight tomorrow?" Riv said. According to him, he laughed at the knight, but I believe his jibe came through rattling teeth.

"I'm not afraid of you, scrawny mouse, this is a lesson I think you're owed. Do you know why they call this place the Taming Chamber?"

"Oh, I remember," Riv told him as the guards were clapping his wrists in new, small chains. He did his share of struggling, but their hands were calloused vices on his forearms. "The Aza-Ondi used to think humans were like animals, unable to do magic, so slow in their movements and speech, so they'd take some of them here to get tamed. Did they miss you when they were training people?"

"Your elders still teach you about it?" the knight asked.

"We have a nursery rhyme, we learned it from the last two Ava-Ondi in our village," Riv said.

"Humans make the day long,

Wash out the pans,

carry the load,

Whip 'em to this song,"

Now, it's important that you know my brother didn't hate humanity, he had several friends he'd dice with, and they were human. No, he hated certain people deeply and for the length of his days, King Hosten, and Sir Grelor's lord, being two, but he didn't hate all humans by far.

The whip was a wild thing in Sir Grelor's hand; he didn't have any kind of art with it, if the marks he left on my brother were any indication. There were as many marks that crossed Riv's arms and back as there were on his thighs and calves.

"Keep them out of the hall," my brother went on, continuing the nursery rhyme we said in secret as children. Our real elders, the Woodlanders who raised us as a village, would scold us harshly when we sung it, but we'd sing it on occasion anyway, because we loved the naughtiness of it, and didn't understand that the rhyme was a theme for oppression. By the time Riv and I were in our adolescence, we came to comprehend it, and sung it no more. On that occasion, he couldn't help himself, so he pressed on. "They're clumsy louts,

bang, thump, clunk, bump,

they will break it all."

"I'll shut you up, you little rat!" Sir Grelor exclaimed as he redoubled his efforts, the whip striking around its target as much as it found its mark. To believe the story the guards told me in a tavern some years later during a chance meeting, Riv actually started laughing as he sung the last part of the rhyme. That singing was interrupted by some wincing when the knight successfully landed a lash or two.

"Put them down, keep them low!

Scatter them all,

Don't let them group,

Put their chiefs in the hole!"

The knight's face was turning red as Riv started the whole thing over again. Sir Grelor was stopped by a man in long robes, who wore around his neck the ceremonial chain of keys, marking him as the head jailer and Master Interrogator, a man who would one day be famous for other persuits, Charthanga. "You'll stop this now, Grelor," he said quietly. The knight only caught a momentary glimpse of a thickly muscled man who stood a head taller than the Master. He seemed to slip into the shadows in the hallway behind Charthanga, and the knight couldn't catch a good look.

"This rat is cheering for humans in slavery! He completely disrespects the knights of the Iron Circle, and therefore decries the rule of our fair King!" Sir Grelor objected.

"He disrespected you, and you'll drown him tomorrow for the entertainment of our Prince and the city," replied the long-haired man. He had a well kept, long beard, it was dark, and his face still youthful, if a little pale. "If you lash him too severely, the sport of the thing will be ruined, and you'll look like a cheat. A weak cheat at that."

"Have it your way, Master Charthanga" Grelor said, throwing the whip across the room. "Listen, rat!" he shouted at Riv. "I'll catch you by the throat and drown you just like I did to your kin during the Liberation."

Riv was quieted by the remembrance of our parents, our aunts, and uncles. Every member of our family was captured and drowned at the feet of King Hosten; none of them were aristocrats, or Ava-Ondi, or well moneyed, but our family was considered dangerous because we all had magical abilities. The only mercies Riv and I had were the extended family of the Woodland District and that we didn't have to watch our parents drown as children. We pictured it often, however, and I still hope that the images in our imaginations are worse than the reality.

As the guards took Riv down, he was eerily quiet and cooperative. I know for near fact that he must have been imagining the drowning of our parents, only I suspect it was by Sir Grelor's hand in his dreadful daymare. They had my brother locked behind his door in his cell when the guards heard him say, "I'm going to kill him tomorrow," and they laughed.

He carefully settled into his corner, where he'd piled old straw and a few scraps of cloth he didn't care to take a close look at. A sudden shifting in the mess sent him back onto his feet. "Shush, you galoot," said Oroza, the dragonling. "Master Nauso slipped me into the cell from that window up there."

"So you're the one they sent?" Riv whispered, settling in beside the tiny dragon.

The young dragonling peered up at him with begging eyes as he squirmed into his lap. "I'm the only one who would fit between the bars. Besides, I have a healing gift, remember? From the sound of things down the hall, the Crusher Duke was a little too late. He's the one who told Master where you were being held. Are you still in one piece after your lashing?"

"That beef-headed knight only got a few good licks in. Why is the Crusher Duke helping me?" Riv asked.

"Your brother made a deal with his mistress, so he came to make sure that you weren't in pieces before your match tomorrow."

Riv was more wounded than he was admitting. By all accounts, the knight had inflicted slowly bleeding wounds distributed across the back of his entire body, more than a dozen, enough to slow anyone down. He winced as he tried to get more comfortable. Sir Grelor may not have been great with a whip, but he made up for it in the number of strikes he took. "You'd think someone like the Crusher Duke could just break me out of here."

"There is a greater game afoot," Oroza said.

"Really? What's going on?"

"I don't know, I just heard Nauso say it, and he told me to be companion to you for as long as I can. I think he did something to unleash my healing talent. I feel a little funny, tired too."

"Sometimes I forget how young you are for a dragon. You were born the same year we were, but you're still a baby, really."

"Baby? I'll show you baby!" he said, snatching Riv's earlobe tightly in his little fingers. He tugged hard, bending Riv's head down awkwardly.

"Okay, ow, ow," Riv complained as quietly as he could manage.

"Apologize," Oroza whispered.

"I'm sorry," Riv said.

"For?"

"Calling you a baby, you're just as old as me."

Oroza let go and settled back into Riv's lap. "Apology accepted."

68

"Well, thank you for coming, I don't know what you're supposed to do for me though, no offense."

"None taken," Oroza said. "Really tired though, maybe I'm supposed to inspire napping?"

"Go ahead and get some sleep, I'll make sure the guards don't spot you," Riv said.

"Thanks. Oh, and I believe you, by the way," Oroza told him, yawning as soon as he finished his affirming comment.

"Believe what?"

"That you'll kill him, of course. That grommy knight has it coming."

"I'm glad someone believes it," Riv replied.

Riv fell asleep moments after Oroza the dragonling drifted off. In fact, he'd never had a better night's sleep. Nauso, my old mentor, had accelerated the dragonling's development a little, so his true nature emerged. He was gifted with healing power, that was true, but it was passive. Oroza was a Luck Drake, who could rejuvenate people he favoured, and he liked few people more than Riv, whom he'd known all his life.

Chapter XI

The crowd had settled in, and, as he expected, most of them seemed to trust that he was taking his story in a direction that they'd enjoy, or at least telling it in a way that wasn't boring. There were a few, especially some of the mentors scattered throughout the crowd, who were being patient but quietly tisking and huffing.

Hallan was one. He sat with arms crossed, one hand occasionally tugging on one side of his thick moustache. You could hide grains of rice in the deep furrows of his brow. Gata was another; her expression was guarded, and she sat stiffly in her seat. Knowing her, she was hoping for a lesson, that a set of morals would find support in his story.

Doril was at Naze's elbow then, whispering. "Bread is being made. Lonen found inspiration in your tale about the lines. He promises there will be enough cheese and nuts in the loaves to 'serve as a wonderful lunch,'" he said, imitating the old Master of the Kitchen's gravelly speech with some accuracy.

"Thank him for me," Naze replied.

"Are you sure you don't want to break for the day? You don't have to tell the entire tale at once."

"Today is the day," Naze said, hoping that his long time apprentice would catch on, would realize that he had been building up to his masterwork. "This will be history, or universally forgotten." Another hint, and he thought he saw a glimmer of realisation in Doril.

Instead of questioning Naze, or trying to further dissuade him, Doril asked, "Do you need anything?"

"No, but I sense that we will have a visitor soon. Please make sure he has something to drink once he's finished his climb. He'll need a very large stein."

"Matthew?" Doril asked, surprised.

Naze only had to nod, and Doril was slipping through the back door to make sure everything would be ready.

The crowd was beginning to speak amongst themselves, and Naze took a moment to close his eyes and fully visualize the next part of his brother's story. It was a time that he could recall very clearly compared to many memories from that part of his life. During his momentary meditation, he found details he thought were gone forever, and after a few moments he was ready to begin the next part of the tale, and the first obvious part of his masterwork.

"When I was young, the realms of Brightwill held this city like a precious gemstone," he said to the crowd, opening his eyes. There was a new strength and presence in his voice that surprised even him. "Many of you are too young to know the city outside as anything more than the ruins left behind by the Cinder War, but I tell you that it was at once marvellous and monstrous. There was opportunity in those days if you were human and could stand the smell. If you were educated, you were in demand. If you were uneducated, your labour was in demand. There were secrets, and treasures to steal, and legends to follow to hidden places if you had the daring inclination. At the centre of all things was the arena, where entertainers sought a place and criminals tried to avoid. The blood, the cheers, the awe-inspiring sights rich patrons commissioned were stranger and more shocking at times than I can tell you. Audiences took their seats expecting the unexpected, and were often well rewarded." Naze raised his hands and brought what was in his memory forth.

All the space at the front of the auditorium was filled with the sight of the Grand Circus in Tribute to Prince Tabbin, or the Ankon Arena as most called it. The illusion was perfect from every angle. No matter where one sat in the auditorium, they could clearly see crowds of people entering, sitting down, and young Naze being ushered in with one such group then finding his seat. The image of young Naze was pushed forward by a human following behind, who was a giant by human standards, over seven feet tall and two feet wide. His sleeveless leather tunic left the collage of tattoos and ritual scars on his arms bare to view. Beside Naze was Rakiz the Betrayer. Only slightly taller than he, she was obviously an Ava-Ondi, or the Old Elven Kind. They were the first to discover magic, according to legend, and they were also the first to sit on thrones, befriend Dragon Kind, and rule men. Rakiz still wore the revealing two-panelled dress, and more jewellery dangled from her, shining silver and gold in the sunlight.

The group made their way through the lowest tier of the arena to a bench only three rows back from the barrier that was to keep the audience away from the arena floor, and keep the entertainers – willing and unwilling – from getting away.

"I can feel your distaste at the image you're seeing," Naze said to everyone watching the scene in the auditorium and the spectacle of young Naze following Rakiz and her human beast, the Crusher Duke. "I can only tell you that I was deeply desperate to save my brother, and I could not imagine how my kindly master, Nauso, or anyone else could help me do that. I was willing to do anything for a chance to save him, and, yes, even though it would break my heart, I would betray anyone to make him safe. The disfavour I sense from you is remarkably similar to the sensation I felt as I walked down to those favoured seats with the Crusher Duke, who killed hundreds of Ondi, and Rakiz the Betrayer, who burned thousands more.

I'm not here to tell you contradictory histories about Rakiz, especially. She would never redeem herself, and I believe history remembers her correctly as a shrewd person who was morally bankrupt for the entire time I knew her. The Crusher Duke and my brother are a different story; history did not favour them, and you'll soon find that there are lies in many historical tomes."

Time advanced a great deal in the image of the arena, as Naze continued. "It was this day that my brother gained his first moniker: The

Woodlander Gremlin, and you'll see how history misremembers him as a frenzied slasher."

Chapter XII

The Arena. To me, the name never did the place justice. Perhaps when it was little more than a royal tourney ground with four stands and when Kamboy was only a town surrounding a castle, then it would have been a good fit. Blood soaked dirt that hosted the entertainments of old had long been buried under layers of history. The dirt was covered by sand and that sand had been turned and changed and turned and changed until grains from all four corners of Brightwill had joined the layers.

Where there were once stands, the Kings of old constructed a building. Atop that oval building were built seats of stone. Tunnels were dug beneath the building an age ago, and over time those tunnels ran deeper and wider than the building above to accommodate dungeons, pens for beasts, secret chambers for the royals, and still more hidden things for well moneyed folk of varied repute. It was the site of a great battle during the Liberation War, where humans and the Ava-Ondi, who ruled them then, faced each other in open combat. It was one of the first true tests of the magic Coriath the Messiah brought to humanity, and I am sure he would have wept if he witnessed it. Coriath was a man of peace, but he saw the imbalance between the humans and their Ava-Ondi rulers. He taught thousands of humans how to use magic to protect themselves, to demonstrate to their overlords that there would be a reckoning if the abuse of power continued. Coriath and the Draconian Justicar, a great dragon named Uthusi, facilitated a charter of rights for the humans with the Ava-Ondi leadership. As soon as Coriath was gone, one of the Ava-Ondi, a High Elf named Surbio, poisoned Uthusi, and imprisoned him deep in their capital, under the Waker Keep. If he knew his acts would serve as a demonstration to humanity on how a centuries old dragon can be bested, I'm sure he wouldn't have followed through with his plan.

With the Draconian Justicar out of the way and Coriath gone, Chifriss, the Ava-Ondi King, tore the charter up and began hunting down Coriath's students. To their surprise, the humans revolted, bringing their new power to bear in earnest. The Liberation War began, and the Culling would follow after only a year, where all Ondi, High Elves, Woodland Elves, and everything in between, would be drowned if they demonstrated any magical ability. A few were able to hide their talents, but the methods of interrogation used by masters like Charthanga were highly effective.

As I took my seat in that arena, I couldn't help but notice the scars of the battle that took place there when I was a child, the one that ultimately led to the Ava-Ondi losing control of the vast realms of Brightwill.

The old, cracked stone barriers that had been erected to protect the crowd had been augmented with a fence of steel that curled down towards the combatants like some broad, needle-toothed maw. The narrow-bodied ancient iron cauldrons had been righted and re-lit at each end of the arena. They stood seven yards high, were surrounded by leaves and strands of jagged iron gilding, a sort of static, sinister plant life, and sported guttering blue flames that cast a clear, ghostly light over most of the tourney ground at night. "It's been years since I've seen a tourney," Carmack said to me, his low voice rattling in my chest. "I gave them up when King Hosten's tastes turned."

"His eldest son is worse, I'm afraid," Rakiz said, "Tabbin is more paranoid than his father, not to mention power hungry and gifted with stunning magic."

"I didn't know he was a practitioner," Carmack, the Crusher Duke, replied.

"He shouldn't be, his father never had a gift for it and his mother was an idiot with no talents whatsoever. His power comes from something else, and he has no mentor. There is some High Elf in him, I'm sure. At one point his forefathers lay with an Ava-Ondi, but you'll never hear him admit it. I've heard even Charthanga deny the possibility of such a thing, and he, above all else, values the truth."

"I was surprised to find him here serving as Prince Tabbin's Master Interrogator. You should be glad to know that Charthanga had no interest in your brother," he said, turning his broad, kindly gaze towards me. "I was in time to stop Sir Grelor from doing Riv any serious harm."

"If Charthanga had no interest in your brother, that most likely means that Riv has no talent for magic," Rakiz said, "Surprising, considering the power your parents had."

"You knew my parents?" I asked.

"Mostly your mother, she was a kind creature, beautiful in the way your people can be, I suppose."

I still had faint memories of my mother. She was the peacekeeper between Riv and me. Her warm smiles and caring embraces were still only a memory away when I was that young. Before I truly knew the world, I could close my eyes and feel her around me, but that comfort was always followed by sadness.

The high born and privileged sects of humans began filing into the arena then. Their servants led the way to ensure the accommodations in the balconies were properly prepared. They brought cushions, rugs, carafes, baskets, bottles, and other creature comforts to make their lords and ladies at home for the day. Watching them dress their spaces in a flurry of sorting and setting was a show unto itself.

The seats reserved for Temple folk were already near full. There was no one I recognized there, but that came as no surprise. It seemed that none of the senior priests, practitioners, or officials would be in attendance. Instead, there were middling members, all hungry to see the object of Temple gossip and report back. Some even had markings from temples at the far ends of the city, most likely taking the opportunity to speak to someone from the High Temple just up the street, where I hoped my people were safely guarded.

As I tried to find someone in the Temple seating far to the right that I could recognize, my attention was drawn away to the seats behind and above as the sounds of heavy steps made the stone under my feet rumble.

The muscular forms of Urgyle Knights, both male and female, were filing in as one unit, represented by an unexpectedly large number.

"What brings the Urgyles here?" I asked, genuinely surprised. They were the first to leave the Middle Kingdom when the Culling began; every Ondi knew them, they were one of the very few Orders of Humans that were still friendly to my people.

Carmack watched until the last of them came out from the entrance tunnel and nodded. "Ninety-eight Urgyles, led by Chrysa herself," he nodded at the broad shouldered, six foot three tall blonde woman sitting at the centre of the host of knights. They didn't wear their armour, but light civilian tunics marked with the sword and wolf emblem. They each carried their long sword though, and carried short handled hammers for close combat. It was a combination they were famous for. She returned the gesture slowly with a tight smile.

"But I thought the Urgyles hated King Hosten," I pressed in a whisper.

"That's why they're here," Carmack answered. "I had a busy night, recruiting for something I hope never happens, young Elf."

"Only eighty-nine turned out," Rakiz said, "Nothing to brag about, really."

Carmack only sighed warily and crossed his arms. "Not like they'd do you any favours. Besides, they're not the only company I met with. Looks like every other order of knights in the county has decided to make a showing." Many had come wearing their armour. A chorus of rattling and sea of shimmers played across the polished grey, silver, gold, red, blue, and green tinted armour as they filed in. The most striking armour was worn by the fewest; a group of nine Draconian Guardians were the last to enter. They wore the armour of the ancient lords, grown of their own bodies using draconian blood magic. The horn and bone plates made little sound. Serpentine flesh held the black, red, dark blue, green, and deep violet suits together, and allowed for a kind of grace and flexibility no other suit could afford its wearer. The armour was the only thing that marked them as part of the same order. They were all different heights, showed signs of different racial lineage, and seemed altogether different in demeanour as well. One stout fellow who had the look of a mountain Ondi, short and broad, smiled and nodded.

"Gronin," Carmack said just loudly enough for the stout knight to hear. "Couldn't keep this quiet, could you?"

"Sorry, once my gob starts waggin'," the gruff man said with a shrug.

"What does that mean? What's going on?" I asked, quietly, looking at the hundreds of knights who had filed in on our side, and then to a greater amount who set up in on the other side of the arena.

"Gronin here was supposed to keep this support effort under his helmet, but somehow the word got out," Carmack explained. "So every other order of knights has turned out, along with their patrons, and their hopeful pledges, and squires. There are three times as many on the King's side of the arena."

"Wouldn't be much of a fight if the other side didn't know when and where it was supposed to happen," Gronin said.

"There wasn't supposed to be a fight at all, you buffoons," Rakiz whispered so harshly that it may as well have been a screech. "This muscle was supposed to be here to lend visual weight to any objections if they had to be made. No one is supposed to draw steel against the Prince. The King loves me well, and I was hoping he'd be here, but if the Prince feels we're pressing against him while his father is ill, things will not go well, to say the least."

"I came for a fight," Gronin replied.

"You're my favourite armed idiot," Carmack said, "but you know boredom will serve us better here."

Gronin sighed and nodded. "You've got too much brain in that head of yours to be called the Crusher Duke. We're here if you need us." He stood and moved to sit closer to his eight companions, who immediately set upon him with questions.

"So, this brother of yours," Chrysa, tall leader of the Urgyles asked me from behind, leaning down so her giant head was whispering right in my ear. "Is he going to provide any contest to Sir Grelor? Are we here to see a good fight at least?"

"Probably not," I answered without giving it a second thought.

"He's small, quick, and wily, you'll see something today," Carmack replied.

"Well, at least they're feeding lions later," Chrysa said, sitting back. "I hear the thieves are particularly nimble today."

"Oh, this is going to be bawdy," Rakiz groaned. "Knights are a loud, crude bunch. Even the women bellow rather than cheer."

The balcony reserved for royalty, set in the centre of the arena, was showing signs of activity. It had its own entrance, and curtains were drawn to hide most of the preparations and entrances, but those curtains rustled, and shapes could be seen moving through the cracks.

The Royal Magi, guards to the King and his family, were first to step to the edge of the balcony and scan the crowd. Their faces were marked with black and red vertical lines that ran over their eyes past either side of their mouths. Chains decorated with tiny foci stones dangled from their ears, and their light tunics flapped in a sudden gust, the deep violet cloth rippling and shimmering. They were humans who fought to serve the King's family, earned their places in the upper magi guilds and were constantly pursuing new avenues to greater power. The highest of them, the High Instructor, was a student of Coriath himself, a disciple who turned his talents to violence during the Liberation War. Only humans were allowed within the ranks of the upper magi guilds, but some of those sorcerers scarcely looked human at all after pursuing the wrong kind of power.

When the pair of Magi were satisfied, a shrill trumpet sounded for a brief note, and dancers rushed the broad tourney floor, trailing red, green, and blue cloth streamers behind.

"I wonder what they'll show us first?" I asked quietly.

Rakiz smiled at me for the first time before answering. "There's the announcements, then an Uterik slaying - that's if whoever they've brought in for entertainment can manage to defeat it this time. They'll treat everyone to some bread while they clean up, then a highland match of some kind-"

"Korben is wresting Tirec today. Doubt there are enough people from my end of the world here to cheer that on properly, mind you," Carmack said.

"Then they're hosting the match between Sir Grelor and your brother," Rakiz finished. "I'm surprised you didn't ask earlier."

"How do you know the events for the day?" I asked.

"A few of the knights I tried to recruit were trying to convince the Prince to hold a grand melee today, but he turned them down. Half the knights here have turned out just to see what this boy likes instead, so the schedule is getting a lot of attention."

I don't know why, but that seemed like the perfect time to ask a question that had been needling me since I met Rakiz and her giant companion. "I hope you don't take offense, it seems like you've gone to a lot of trouble, but how are all these knights, or even you, going to help my brother? The situation still seems impossible. Are you going to rush the arena and fight the guards to get him out? That would start a war, I'm sure, and not even I'd like to see that."

"I would!" Gronin shouted from where he sat, a bench to our left.

"I think my brother would too, but that's not the point," I replied.

"No," Rakiz replied. "Your brother still has to win, or at least earn the mercy of the crowd. Then we can shout down a potential kill order, and at best disgrace Sir Grelor. His Order would definitely demote him for his behaviour if it resulted in dishonour. Human commoners don't like bullies of any height, and, as you can see, there are a lot coming in."

She was right; even more humans were moving in by the dozen, slowly filling the twenty-eight thousand seats in the oval. My heart broke at the stark reality that my brother would face a real knight in combat. He was a magnificent Wayist fighter, quick, smart, and so agile, but his style depended on having things to climb, to leap from. Half of his practice seemed to be spent off the ground, jumping, swinging, and perching, the kind of talents I never mastered. The arena floor was flat for what seemed an endless span, and all of the weapons Riv had trained with were small, not great big soldier's tools like the ones humans used. To everyone who hated Ondi, and most did, it would be a comedy. To the few who still loved the Elven people, especially our darker skinned kind, it would be another tragedy.

That was the end of the conversation. Everyone knew that piling reassurances onto me would only make things worse, force me to think about what was about to happen. While we sat and watched Vurrio the Great, a showman with a long hooked pike, defeat the giant insect utterking effortlessly I was drifting between dread and anger.

As the carcass of the massive insect was carried away in several pieces, bread was brought out. A silent contract had been signed between the audience and the throwers, where the bread would stop flying through the air if too many people were unseated. The loaves, each large enough to feed two, were tossed from the aisles, over the tall fence from the arena floor and from behind us.

Carmack took two loaves when Rakiz turned hers down and when the basket boy had gone he handed the second to me. I refused at first but Carmack took it for me and dropped it into my lap. There would be two more offerings of bread: one just as the sun started its journey down from its apex and another as it was about to disappear over the horizon. I expected that I would see neither, since I was certain that my brother would be dead long before.

With great fanfare, the wrestling match began. Each man had his own style, I suppose you'd call it. Korben was announced by a flute and horns while Tirec was thundered in by drums. They were much older than I expected, comically large men with grey in their oiled hair. Old men who were there more for the coin than the spirit of competition, it seemed. They put on a good show, but guarded themselves from injury. There were slow, powerful looking punches, quick tripping attempts, and grapple manoeuvres. All of it was interspersed with posturing that was better performed than the wrestling itself, of which there was comparatively little. When it was all said and done, there was no blood on the sand, but Tirec had pinned a red faced Korben down in an awkward contortionist's twist.

After feigning some difficulty at recovery, they both took their turn at bowing for the crowd. Not many coins were thrown at their feet, and each suffered his fair share of boos. They left through the same portcullis, no sign of animosity visible between the pair. They would be on their way to another arena or tourney to entertain other crowds. I could tell from Carmack's restless shifting that it left him wanting, and Rakiz spent the entire match with her eyes closed, meditating, I assumed.

I tucked most of my bread away, in the folds of my shirt. I fully expected all my opportunities and newfound friends to disappear the moment my brother was cut down, and making food last was a deeply ingrained reflex. I wouldn't think any less of them for leaving after my brother died. How was I special? Rakiz saw some potential in me as a magical practitioner, but there were many young Ondi-Ne who were just as promising. Carmack had been kind to me since I met him over a breakfast of fruit and porridge that morning in the Temple, but I never forgot that he slew hundreds of Ava-Ondi, perhaps not my kind specifically, but Ava-Ondi were still very similar to Ondi-Ne; we were still both Elf Kind. I heard he even killed two dragons while commanding a company of knights, and glimpsing the scars between his tattoos, I could believe it. No, I didn't expect that Rakiz or Carmack would be long time companions, or that they could be trusted. I was there because my other options were even more hopeless, and, if the only way I could see my brother again was from that seat, I wasn't moving.

The caller took the stand beneath the King's box. His barrel chest puffed out, filling with air, then his voice boomed across the crowd. I didn't understand why two practiced wrestlers, and a match between a knight and a fearsome insect-beast four times his size didn't draw the same size of audience my brother and Sir Grelor did. At a glance I could see people were bringing all their socializing and moving about to a halt, and taking their seats with anticipation. Surely the rare match between a human warrior I'd never heard of and a giant cockroach was more interesting, and a lot less one-sided.

Commoners of several races, mostly human, cheered as if they knew what the announcer was about to say, drowning him out at first. He waved his arms and put his finger across his lips to silence the crowd.

I caught a glimpse of the Prince in the royal box above him, nestled in a pile of furs, behind heavy curtains that were drawn just enough for him to see the arena floor. He looked as if the heat of the day didn't affect him in the least. In fact, with his alabaster skin and a pile of fine furs atop him on a great throne, it looked as though he was quite cold.

The speaker beneath the royal box tried to speak again, his voice augmented by an enchantment that ensured that the sound would carry to everyone in the arena that time. I looked a little closer and realized that it was the Amblinton Market Crier, who had seen where the story of the match began with his own eyes.

"A boy, no more than a tenth of a man in stature, was taking his temple bread when the valorous knight and his company entered the Amblinton Temple Square. They only wanted the same bread as the poor who had gathered; a testimony to their vigour in service, their hunger was. A fair request, since Sir Grelor and his company were on their way to patrol the outer walls for the King. One must take sustenance before embarking on such an arduous mission.

"When the boy, Riv of the Woodland District, saw the knight take his place in the line, he objected. 'This bread isn't for you!' he shouted as he threw stones. The valiant knight, assuming anyone of honour would cease their assault to parley, removed his helmet to reveal himself but that only encouraged Riv. Riv the runt, the lowborn boy of no house, took it upon himself to assail the knight with insults and stones only because he wished to partake of bread with the common and slake his thirst. Sir Grelor could have cut him down at his leisure, but no, his sword remained in its sheath. When the city guard drew swords and nocked arrows, ready to slay the small wildling who disrupted all the lines, extending the hunger of the crowd, Sir Grelor bid them stay their arms. It was then that the great Wizard Chonolo entranced Riv, who surrendered himself under his wise direction. He knew that honour must be satisfied, and being a veteran of the arena himself, Chonolo suggested a match.

"Despite the low birth and unfortunate breeding of the cruel spirited Riv, Sir Grelor agreed to do the mutt boy the honour. Who could refuse such a request from the High Wizard Chonolo, after all?"

I couldn't resist but rip the heel from the loaf tucked away in my shirt and throw it as hard as I could towards the caller. It didn't make it, but the intention was clear to everyone watching. Most of the Urgyle Knights behind me thought it was hilarious. Some in the crowd gasped, others laughed, and yet another cried, "That's not how it happened!" and pieces of bread began to sail through the air at the crier, who was protected by an unseen barrier.

The crier only gave pause for a moment, then pretended as though nothing was amiss. "That brings us here today, to see the good, lordly Sir Grelor deliver on his promise to face the wild, grotesquely crossbred Riv before as many witnesses as the city could present. To enrich our entertainment, we're presenting this as a retelling of one of our own folk tales, that of the Goblin and the Knight, wherein a diabolical creature creeps into a village to steal children so he can raise them into more goblins for the demon horde. Here he is, playing the part of the little demon, the lowborn who would see our valourous knights starve: Riv the Gremlin!"

The bread stopped flying as double portcullis gates were drawn apart like black iron teeth at one end of the arena. Cheers mixed with equal parts laughter as Riv emerged with his arms raised. He had been stripped nude, and painted, or more likely dipped, in green paint. His grin was bright in contrast to the dark shade; he behaved as though he was a glorious challenger, a favourite, and his enthusiasm added to the uproarious mirth of the crowd.

"Oh my curses and blessings!" Rakiz uttered in shock as she opened her eyes. "That's, well, that's so utterly-" She shook her head and left her objection incomplete.

Carmack was grinning from ear to ear. "What is it?" I asked him over the din.

"He's already winning the crowd. A lot of the people laughing now will cheer for him later."

I glanced to my left, where Gronin and his Draconian Guardians were already on their feet, cheering vigorously, grinning broadly. The Urgyles were next to take to their feet, pounding the stone stands with their heavy feet and calling, "Champion! Champion! Our Champion comes!" over and over again. No one joined in on their call, but thousands began cheering at my brother, for reasons I did not yet understand. I thought he was playing the fool, nimbly back flipping and cartwheeling, giving everyone an eyeful, which I suspected was his intention. "A brat to the end," I muttered.

Carmack chuckled and stood, his baritone roar adding its power to the cry of "Champion! Champion! Our Champion comes!" He reached down and pulled me onto my feet by the shoulder. Not knowing what my voice could add to the commotion, I joined in on the chant, and within a few heartbeats I was screaming it so hard that it brought tears to my eyes. Commoners were beginning to pick up the chant, and to my disbelief, the sound of it rung in my ears more loudly than any other noise, even the worrying thumping of those brute knights behind us.

Riv was walking to the centre of the arena waving both hands and smiling at the audience. As he bowed to the royal box , then turned and bowed in the opposite direction, causing a wave of covered eyes and turned heads amongst the royals, he burst into laughter. My brother, who at first glance looked like a speck on the sand, was already larger than life.

"Presenting the honourable-" the caller began, stopping for a moment in hopes that his voice would stop the chanting of the crowd.

Riv's eyes went wide and he turned towards the announcer with his finger pressed to his lips. He turned towards the bulk of the stadium then and cupped his hands behind his ears. The respondent cheer was deafening. I couldn't hear myself even though the straining in my throat told me that I would surely become a mute if I tried to shout any harder. The frenzy of the majority of that crowd was unlike anything I had seen, or have seen since. "Champion! Champion!" called so many that I was sure they would hear it across Brightwill, along both Eastern and Western shores.

In an exaggerated gesture, Riv covered his mouth with both hands, then turned, and sat down, looking up at the announcer. He gestured for him to proceed with both arms outstretched as the audience quieted on his comical command.

"Presenting the honourable, shining knight, playing the part of the Goblin Slayer in our tale, Sir Grelor!" the caller shouted. He only remained on his stand for a moment longer before retreating, shaking his head.

The knight and his horse were fully dressed in gleaming plate. The only thing missing from the image was a lance. The commoners were the majority, and it showed as their jeers and boos outdid any supportive stomping or cheering. The crowd was against him, and I still didn't know why. I believed that human children were regaled by tales of knights and princesses, honourable heroes who slew dragons and killed tyrant elven rulers. I'd heard some of the ridiculous stories myself, where evil Ava-Ondi Queens tricked fair maidens into traps that were anything but cunning, and mutton-headed knights rode to their rescue, somehow killing the powerful Queen with a slash of their sword, and saving the fair maiden. How humans of all ages were cheering for my brother was anything but plain to me until Carmack spoke. "The Middle Kingdom's common people have been looking for a hero for a long time. Your brother doesn't look like an Ava-Ondi, even though he's as small as one. But, look, his face is wide, he doesn't look as serious as the Ava, like she always does," he said, regarding Rakiz. "He is more a spirit on the sand than a competitor, and it's a kind given to rejoicing."

"He's bloody hilarious!" Gronin the Knight said as he moved to our bench. "And these folks need that almost as much as they need a full belly now that they've realized that the new human King is no better to them than the Ava-Ondi were. The new tyrants may be taller, but they're not much different."

"Many of them can recognize that he is not Ava-Ondi, but Ondi-Ne," Rakiz said. "The Ondi-Ne have never taken thrones in Brightwill. They only fight when they must, and are drawn back to their woods by their very nature. To wise humans, the Ondi-Ne are the old spirits, representing the woodland that once covered Brightwill, and they are vanishing, just like the trees. I'll tell you the stories humans share about you sometime. I hope we're about to witness the birth of another folktale today."

"A lot of words that mean that your brother there is about to become a hero or a martyr," Carmack said. "Because there's nothing like an underdog, and they've probably never seen anyone so disadvantaged as him."

Sir Grelor stopped a few yards from the gate and dismounted, a pair of squires dressed in freshly polished footman's chainmail took his shield and led his horse back through the portcullis. It closed behind them with a shrill clanking.

The crowd started to calm a little, and the sounds of stomping feet, bracers striking breastplates or sword pommels, along with the shouts of the Knightly Orders seated on the other side of the arena were starting to overtake the more common noise. There was a threat implied to the common folk in such displays, and I was familiar with it. The Knightly Orders, the Circle of Armour that was promised to protect the King and the Realm, didn't seem to be paying much attention to their Champion, as much making a torrent of noise that was directed at the Urgyle Knights and Draconian Guardians.

"These sods want to see a chestful of armour?" Carmack asked no one in particular as he started pulling off his tunic. "They want to see what a real man wears when he's off to a battle?" His chest, sides, back, and arms were covered in the ink of a dozen nations. There were magical images, runes, marks of honour, and even a few noted failures. At the centre was the coin stamp of his house, a sceptre and mace crossed over the eye of a dragon. Scars interrupted some of the art, while a few of the fresher markings were drawn around permanent blemishes. I couldn't help but notice that some of the lettering in the images on the man's chest were Onde-Ne in origin, and I wished Carmack would stop moving so much so I could read them.

"I'm guessing you want the glamour removed?" Rakiz asked, laying her hand on his face for a moment. Tattoos and scars on his face and neck were revealed, a fearsome design that looked like his skull was on the outside, etched with ancient words and symbols of significance. I could feel very real power in the markings on his body; nothing was for decoration, his armour was etched onto his skin.

He was a loud, monstrous thing as he got to his feet and bellowed open mouthed, "I see you! Riv of the Ondi-Ne! I see you!" His arms went up, his shouting brought forth similar demonstrations from the few countrymen in the crowd. Anyone who recognized Carmack as a hero cheered for Riv anew, ignoring even the opposing knights, who redoubled their efforts to drown out the wild man across from them.

Riv spotted them, pointed and waved excitedly. He jumped as high as he could several times before he came down and feigned modesty, as though he had just realized then that he was nude. The crowd that cheered him burst into laughter at his antics and rooted anew when the jest ended.

Sir Grelor wasn't pleased. Even with his helmet on, his cadence betrayed him as he began to march towards the centre, and Riv.

Riv's response was as surprising as it was comical. He started to cross the distance with his head cocked and arms open wide, offering a relatively broad embrace with his thin arms.

The gleaming knight drew his sword in one expert sweep before half the distance was closed and Riv yelped and jumped backwards, comically feigning fear. The audience's laughter dwindled before long, and was not replaced by cheering as it was before.

"He's going to disgrace himself," I overheard a knight behind me say.

The auditorium quieted as Sir Grelor drew a dagger from his belt and tossed it on the sand between himself and Riv. It could be seen as a gesture, an honourable knight arming his opponent so there was more of a challenge. I didn't trust Grelor, and I uttered, "Don't pick it up."

Riv slowly approached the weapon. Rakiz cringed and shielded her eyes with her hand.

Sir Grelor lowered his sword and gestured at Riv with his free hand, inviting him to pick up the dagger. "Don't pick it up!" I shouted. The dagger was too close to Sir Grelor; I was sure my brother would be halved the moment he bent down.

Carmack must have shared the thought. "Leave it be! Retreat!" he bellowed.

Riv looked up as he started stooping. It was too late.

The knight's savage backhand slice came and Riv wasn't ready. On pure reflex he fell backwards, losing a lock of hair to the sharp edge. He scrambled out of range as Sir Grelor lunged forward with a speed that seemed unimpeded by the weight of his armour.

Having missed his broad stroke, he kicked Riv in the stomach. Riv was sent rolling across the sand and to everyone's surprise he came up on his feet, unsteady, but just in time to barely sidestep another sweep of the towering knight's sword. He staggered backwards in his haste to get away. The tip of Sir Grelor's blade caught shallow purchase across Riv's thigh, driving him back even faster.

The commotion in the vast audience rose and fell with each movement in the attack, rising to a cheer as Riv rolled back to his feet with Sir Grelor at his back and broke into a run. He didn't look back until he was halfway across the broad arena floor.

Watching Riv as he put a great deal of distance between him and the knight before turning around and running backwards gave me time to fear the obvious outcome of the match more than ever. Sir Grelor was a trained fighter, tall, of old human stock, and tried in battle. It didn't matter that he was much slower, that his armour must have been like an oven in the bare sunlight; that was a knight chasing my brother, and eventually Riv would misstep or get overconfident. Then, it would be over.

Sir Grelor was well behind, and it remained thus. Riv's thigh wasn't bleeding profusely, and he hadn't taken to limping, so it musn't have been a great injury. He was, in fact, jogging lightly backwards around the broad arena's edge. Without thinking, without realizing at first, he was stirring the crowd into a frenzy. As he passed, the commoners were throwing pieces of bread at his feet. A few nobles even tossed small copper and silver coins.

He stuffed a few of the morsels of bread into his mouth, and then, when he finished chewing, he popped a few of the coins in after. The crowd found that funny, but I knew he'd be fishing after the money later if he survived. His stomach was the only pocket he had, after all.

Riv bowed whenever he noticed someone throwing money, all while running backwards and glancing at the knight regularly. This ignited a fire in Sir Grelor, who redoubled his efforts at catching his quarry. With one eye on his pursuer, Riv seemed to know it was time to quit his playing, but left the crowd roaring with laughter as he acted surprised at the knight's redoubled efforts, flinging a few pieces of bread into the air in feigned panic and continued his run.

"He certainly knows how to buy time," Rakiz said, an honest note of appreciation in her voice. "If he keeps this up, and Sir Grelor kills Riv, he'll forever be known as his murderer. Never mind whatever he may accomplish in the future, this will overshadow everything." She turned to me then. "I'm sorry, I shouldn't speak so casually."

I shook my head. "I can see what's going on, speak plainly. But I wonder..." I hesitated, watching as my brother neared my section of the stadium at a casual run. "Is there actually a chance the crowd will call for him to be spared?"

"A good chance at this rate, but it would take a member of the royal family to stop the match," Carmack informed me. "Here he comes, make a ruckus!" He lept to his feet, put his arms in the air and cheered as loudly as he could manage.

"Set him free!" shouted someone beneath us. Another shouted it, and in seconds it became a chant.

Riv's gaze passed over the dozens between him and me, and when our gazes met, Riv gave a definitive nod. His expression was deadly serious in that moment, and when his eyes moved past, it regained a measure of its mirth, but not all. There was a new resolve in my brother, and I couldn't begin to fathom what it would lead to.

A token was thrown down, a bunched up embroidered lady's kerchief, and Riv snatched it up. I saw a young woman at the other end of the King's box bounce up and down with glee. She looked to be mostly

Ondi-Un, a descendant of Dwarves, but mixed with human enough to be a little taller. Her padded seat was set among many that encircled the Prince's section of the large balcony. One of her betters chided her into being seated.

Riv kissed the white kerchief as he maintained his fair pace around the arena and held it up for the crowd to cheer over. I barely heard him shout; "I'm sorry, fair lady!" with all his might, but couldn't fathom what he was apologizing for.

Could it be that he knew he was doomed, and he'd never be able to return her affection? Was he sorry that he had to keep running, and couldn't introduce himself properly? No, I discovered it was neither of these as he stopped suddenly, and held his manhood in one hand, and the fine kerchief in the other.

That silenced the entire arena. I swear I could hear his stream, which was surprisingly plentiful, strike his hand and that bunched up token, which he kept in the path of his urine with great care.

He looked over his shoulder, and when he realized that even Sir Grelor had stopped in his tracks, his helmeted head cocked, he carefully turned around to face the knight. Keep in mind: my brother was closest to the royals as he was doing this, and the young woman who sent her token down to the arena floor to him was turning every shade of pink and red at the sight of Riv relieving himself on it. Just as a few boos and other discontented sounds were beginning to rise from the crowd, Riv, my brother the goblin, waggled his manhood, which was not so considerable that everyone in the arena could see the act, but not shameful in size by far, at Sir Grelor, who was immediately enraged. He sprinted at my brother as best as he could, who cackled as he ran, cupping the desecrated token of affection in both hands.

I recall worrying at how slow Riv was running in comparison to his earlier efforts, but didn't for long. He made it past the dagger Sir Grelor had dropped for him, then turned, his expression perfectly placid.

Sir Grelor closed the distance at a dead run and swung his massive sword in an arc that Riv leapt over effortlessly. At the apex of his height he tossed the soiled kerchief at the knight, covering his helm.

The knight did not reel back, but attempted an overhead swing instead, and missed. Riv jumped onto Sir Grelor, snatched the kerchief from where it was falling down the Kknight's helm and stuffed it into the warrior's visor. "You wanted a gremlin?" he screeched fiercely.

Before the knight's hands caught him, Riv was on the sand, running to the dagger. Sir Grelor struggled to get the kerchief from his helm, dropping his sword in doing so. My brother didn't hesitate as he slashed the backs of Sir Grelor's knees, causing the knight to stumble, but there was no blood, or sign that the blade was at all effective. I swear I could see my brother mouth the word, 'dull!' from where I sat, and Riv took the next step.

He walked around the Knight, speaking to him with an expression that was at the same time angry and disgusted. With a wild grab, Sir Grelor caught Riv by the waist with both hands. Whatever he planned to do next didn't matter, Riv was close enough to jab the dagger's point into Grelor's visor, and he was free.

Riv let the dagger go, Grelor fell to his knees as he reached for the hilt, and my brother leapt up, and grabbed the front of the knight's breastplate. The crowd was in a frenzy, on their feet, screaming and cheering as my brother easily pulled Grelor down face first onto the sand. To my disbelief, Riv was out from under the falling knight before he could be crushed beneath the man and his armour. In the next instant, Riv was hopping onto the back of the knight's head, the fallen man's legs twitched as he jumped up and down on the back of his helmet, making sure his enemy was dead.

He continued until the portcullis gates opened, and the crowd was silenced, and I couldn't help but mutter, "Now they're going to execute him."

Chapter XIII

Naze could feel the energy from the Enduring Light begin to seep into him. The artefact he hid in a fold of his robe was not good or evil; it was only a source of power left behind by Coriath himself. No one would be able to sense it on him at the podium yet, though by the time the sun sank down beneath the horizon, it would be obvious to every experienced practitioner in the auditorium that his raw power was building, but that wouldn't be for many hours yet. The first of the kitchen crew were arriving at the rear entrances with loads of bread.

He let the illusion of the arena fade and smiled at the disappointed groans. "It's time to have a bit of lunch, I'll return shortly," he announced. There was someone he had to speak to, someone who had a vested interest in how he told his brother's story.

When he turned around, Doril was already holding the curtain behind him open. Beneath the broad performance dais at the front of the auditorium was a sitting room, somewhere for people to wait until it was their turn to appear on stage. Most recently it was used for a play, and there were still garish costumes hanging along the walls. One mask with a long nose and devilishly shaped eye holes seemed to stare at Naze, silently taunting. He casually turned it so it faced the wall before sitting down in one of the older padded chairs.

"He's here," Doril said. "I'll get some tea and a bit of that bread."

"Thank you, Doril, make sure you get some for Matthew as well," Naze replied.

"Thank you, Master," replied a gentle, low voice as he ducked into the room. The door was a little short for the fair-haired man, he was only two inches shorter than the Crusher Duke when he was in his prime.

"You're looking well," Naze said, starting to stand.

Matthew motioned for him to remain seated, and Naze complied. He took a stone seat for his chair and smiled a little at the old man. It was discouraging for Naze to see Matthew's young face look so weary. It looked like he could sleep for a week, and the wear on his thick hide armour suggested that he'd had a hard journey. "In one piece, no thanks to the Cull Scroungers. Tribes of them down there in the old districts now, killing anyone they don't recognize for easy meat."

"So Brightwill is getting worse," Naze said, leaning back in his chair.

"South Haven is gone, got rushed by Risen and the Scrounge Lords. This is the only refuge on the eastern side of Brightwill," Matthew said. He took a long drink from a water skin and capped it. "There are no cities left between here and Turhall, and people are starving there."

"Any news from Steadshore?" Naze asked.

Doril brought a tray with bread and a tea service without the kettle. There was a large cup for Matthew, and a set of smaller cups for the Ondi-Ne in the room. The large, steaming clay kettle was on a trolley behind, wheeled by a pair of older students who regarded Matthew with quiet awe. They had never seen a human like him, heavily muscled and road worn, with a large hammer and scabbarded sword crossing his back. Matthew nodded his thanks to Doril, picked the largest loaf of cheesy bread for himself and took a large bite.

Naze was on edge waiting for him to finish. The man was like his father, the man once famous as the Crusher Duke, in many ways, and he often took his time to answer a question, especially an important one. When he was finished chewing and swallowing, he nodded. "Steadshore is still busying itself with trade, just not with anyone from Brightwill. It seems everyone has given up on these realms. A few ships from Brightwill do get through the fleet guarding Steadshore's coast, but fewer and fewer. The Risen have begun invading across the ocean, in Urikel and Leese, in the south, no one knows who brought them. No one has named the necromancer responsible. I'd be asking you for help assassinating him if I had a name, but this one has learned from Charthanga's mistakes, I'll bet. Won't be easy to put down."

Naze looked to the pair of older students and nodded. "Thank you," he said, and they took that as their signal to leave. He waited until he sensed they were well down the hall and out of earshot before continuing the conversation. "Do you think you could find enough ships to transport everyone in this refuge to Steadshore if you had to?"

"Knew you were going to ask that," Matthew said, shaking his head. "Won't be easy, we'd have to trade everything for passage with the Companies, and that's assuming I can get a small ship close enough to signal the Augin Fleet. Could be done though, but I'd need some of your best to keep us hidden along the way, or to burn anyone who got in our way."

"But it could be done?"

"Most would make it, but some would die fighting. Can't move this many people without drawing a lot of attention, and a lot of them haven't seen the world since the last of the unwalled cities burned in Brightwill. Why? Your plan not working?"

"It is, but we need contingencies, backup plans," Naze said. He was having difficulty ignoring Doril who he was sure was holding a number of questions in reserve as he stared into his teacup.

"All right, I'll start putting a plan together tomorrow. Got a question for you, though," Matthew said, tucking a strand of long blonde hair back into his ponytail.

"Anything," Naze replied.

"Are you going to clear my father's name while you tell them the truth about Riv? I'd like people to know he wasn't the Crusher Duke by choice, even if it's something you keep for the end."

"They'll know, my dear boy, don't worry," Naze said.

"I'm off then, going to make a bed out of a couple benches and let your story fill my head. Been a while since I've seen my da."

"Matthew," Naze said, standing. Even on his feet he was barely a third the height of the large human. "Thank you. You've ranged and gathered for us most of your life, and I can't thank you enough, especially since the hardest work may be yet to come."

"Better than hiding here for me, think I'd go mad if I were stuck behind walls," Matthew said with a tired smile. "You're welcome just the same though."

Naze sat down and took a sip of his hot tea. He was keenly aware that Doril waited until Matthew was well past the doorway before he began his interrogation. "Leaving the refuge if your plan doesn't turn out?" he asked. "Details, I need details."

"My masterwork is underway," Naze said. The statement brought relief, the pressure of keeping secrets from his best friend was lifting. "This story, the way I'm telling it and where it will lead, is a large part of it. The preparation, if you will."

"For thirty years you've kept the nature of your masterwork secret, and you managed to keep me in the dark. What is your goal here, Naze?"

"I'm going to set Brightwill on a new course. Put the demon horde down, set the continent's feet back on the path to civilization."

"With one masterwork you're going to defeat the Risen? Others have tried grand magical feats that were supposed to banish all the demons; it's led to the destruction of the sorcerer every time. *Every time*, mind you."

"None have had all the tools I've gathered, my experience, or my connection to the origins of the Risen. I am uniquely qualified for this, and it will work. Will I be alive when midnight comes? Perhaps not, that's the only variable. Something will be consumed by the end, and it may very well be me. I'm hoping it will be this instead," he said, fishing the ring out of his pocket. "I have the Enduring Light; its power should stand in for me in the end, but if it doesn't, I'll sacrifice this life so Brightwill can shine again."

"I would put myself in your place if I could, if it would prevent any harm from befalling you," Doril said, reaching out to touch the gleaming ring but stopping short.

"I know, that's why I've kept my secrets, Doril. It must be me, and I didn't want our last years together to be plagued by arguments about sacrifice and destiny. You are a bright point in my life."

"Thank you," Doril said. "You know I've always loved you, even during the wars. Especially during the wars."

Open affection had been rare between them for so long, it gave Naze pause. The care they had for each other didn't need to be expressed, but hearing it aloud resurrected old feelings that only fortified the bond he felt with Doril. "I know, and I have to do this, because life isn't worth living for anyone in the refuge if I don't at least try."

"If you fail, we'll be noticed. There's no way around it, and we'll have to face everything out there without you."

"That is why you and Matthew will lead everyone to Steadshore. The Empress will embrace the Amber Order if you can make landfall there. You will have to fight your way east, through cannibal tribes and Risen alike, then find ships to make your crossing. He's right, the Companies may help us, but not without trading a few of our best wizards for a time. The rest of the details Matthew and his rangers will make plain to you, and I believe they'll stay with you the entire way. But that's all last resort, 'if the worst should happen' thinking. I won't fail today, the future will brighten."

"I believe in you," Doril said, putting his cup down and standing.

Naze followed his lead, and accepted a close embrace.

"I'll miss you if this doesn't take that bauble instead," Doril said.

"Nothing completely dies," Naze reassured.

Chapter XIV

By the time Naze took the podium again, the auditorium audience had finished their lunch and settled in. The sun was high in the sky, and Naze was grateful for the north wind gusting through the tall arched windows surrounding the audience.

His power was growing, he could feel each person in the room simply by opening his mind, and soon he would be able to touch the elements themselves. The Enduring Light was an artefact like few others, a bottomless well of power, and it took discipline to maintain mastery over it.

The younger members of his audience had been warned about the graphic nature of the next portion of the story by their betters, Naze could sense it, but he could also feel that they were ready. The horrors that the children had seen before arriving in the Amber Refuge far surpassed what most instructors and mentors expected. There were few things that Naze could show them that would shock or horrify, which was a relief, since that wasn't his goal at all. He intended to move them, to draw them in emotionally. How the instructors knew that there was something horrific coming up was no mystery to Naze. Most of them knew the general outcome of the story he was telling, but few knew the details.

He gestured for the podium to be removed, and several students in their teens rushed it backstage. Fitful gusts of wind caught his robes as he raised his hands and brought the image of Riv standing alone in the great arena to life in front of everyone. "My brother is about to learn that victory doesn't always lead to peace, freedom, or wealth."

* * *

He stood atop the steel-clad back of the large human knight's corpse, painted green except for his gleaming white smile. The masses gathered in the arena were in a cheering frenzy at my brother's sudden turn of fate.

Even from where I was sitting I could tell that the idea that he won was just starting to dawn on him, and he paid attention to the two thirds of the audience that was cheering, bowing and pumping his fists in the air.

I was more concerned with the audience members who weren't cheering, those knights and well dressed patrons sitting across the arena from us. "Now they'll execute him," I said.

"I don't know, not for sure," Carmack said, "but we're about to find out."

The crier stepped into his box and raised his hands, signalling the celebrating audience to be silent. They complied after a moment, and even Riv looked up at him from the sand of the arena. "As is his right as the patron of these games, your Prince would address you on behalf of his father, the King. I am honoured to present his Royal Highness, Prince Tabbin." I knew him as the son of the man who drowned my parents and all of my other relatives. Many of us hoped that King Hosten's son would take the throne back then, and relax the laws suppressing the Ondi, myself included.

The crier stepped back and looked to the balcony above and to his left. Prince Tabbin emerged from between heavy curtains. His skin was alabaster white, and he looked so thin even I thought he looked emaciated and sickly. His features were sharper than I'd seen in a human, with a pointed chin and nose, a long face, and pale eyes. I looked to Rakiz, who nodded and whispered, "My sister's son. She bewitched the King and had him in secret. He was revealed to the King two years ago."

She didn't have to say any more to flare my suspicions. The King took sick around the same time, and I secretly found myself hoping that this alabaster skinned Prince was somehow responsible for the man's death or imprisonment. In hindsight, I can say I rarely met an Ava-Ondi I felt I could trust, or that was even particularly likeable back then. They seemed to see themselves as a race above us, but there was a little flame of hope kindled in me at the thought that they may be taking over again. At least they'd let my people, the Ondi-Ne, do as they liked. It was a small-minded attitude, that came from little experience in the world, but those were the opinions that coloured my decisions.

The appearance of the Prince brought fewer cheers than my brother. "Little gremlin, congratulations on your surprising victory," the Prince said, his reedy voice shrill to my ears. "I am pleased to award you with your freedom and two gold sovereigns, but I caution you that I have been commanded not to restrict the actions of his knights if their champion were to lose. Having said that, congratulations, and long life to you, little woodland child."

He retreated to his private balcony, and his servants began disassembling the curtains, the gilding, the rods holding up the temporary roof, and the plush seating around the throne with great haste. The crowd was silent, and the tension was palpable.

"He stirs the pot and takes his leave," Rakiz spat under her breath. "He'd be so much stronger if my sister was alive."

"What does that mean?" I asked as I looked to my brother on the arena floor, then across the sands to seats where dozens of shining knights sat with their footmen and squires. They were filing out of their seats with surprising haste, entering the bowels of the arena.

"The knights are going to present your brother with his sovereigns, then they'll have their way with him," Carmack said. "That's unless we guard him." He turned to look behind him, then to his right. A silent nod was all he had to offer to get his friends on their feet. "Are you ready to move quickly, Naze?" Rakiz asked.

"Yes," I replied, my heart pounding so quickly I feared it would burst. I was nervous, wished more than anything that Nauso, or Maydo, or any of my elders were there.

"We're going first," Rakiz said. I felt a surge of power burst from her, and we were in the air, flying over the barricades between us and the arena sands. Carmack, his short dragon-bone armoured friend, and all of his knights were with us as we dropped onto the sand. Swords, axes, and hammers were drawn, and I rushed to my brother. "The King's knights, they're coming to kill you," I told him, answering his confused expression.

He kicked Sir Grelor's head with his heel, then pried the dagger from his head. "Those whoresons, I've never known a knight with honour."

"Oi! I'm Gronin," the Draconian Guardian's Captain said over his shoulder as he joined the circle surrounding me and Riv. "Honour is all I have other than this armour and my blades, boy. I'll introduce myself properly later. You're right about these whoresons though, the King they pledge to hates all you wee kind, looks like his son doesn't give a damn either."

Even surrounded by nine Draconian Guardians, the Crusher Duke, and Rakiz, I couldn't feel safe. The audience cheered at the promise of a spontaneous event, commoner and well moneyed alike. There was no trace of the Prince; the last of his servants were hurrying off as I glanced up.

Chrysa, in shining armour, with a hammer in one hand and an axe in the other, led her Urgyle Knights onto the arena sands through the east gate. Her hundred made the floor beneath our feet rumble, and I thought we were well saved until I heard my brother's withering tone. "Oh, shit," he said, wringing the hilt of his dagger with both hands.

I followed his gaze west and realized that the rumbling floor was caused as much by the King's knights, charging from the opposite gates. "Let's cull the weak," Rakiz said as she hurled a wave of yellow and red flame at the knights charging twenty abreast through the arena portcullis.

The flames turned sand to glass, and I expected the smoke to clear, revealing a grisly sight, but to my surprise, every one of them emerged unharmed. "The King must be spending a great deal for his armourers to cast flame wards on every breastplate," Carmack said. "Looks like this will take some real work."

Riv poised to fight, and I shot him a look that must have made my irritation and disbelief plain. "We're not fighters, what are we supposed to do here?" I asked Rakiz and anyone else who was listening.

It was my brother who answered. "It's times like these I wish our people were great burrowers," he said, brandishing the dull knife his last opponent gave him, "Or had wings like the Ondi-Isi."

"We're all dead unless we focus on fighting as a unit," Chrysa said, "Only attack if you see an obvious opening, other than that, stay out of the way."

The notion that I was in the heart of danger became very real to me then. "Why don't we just float up and away?" I asked Rakiz, who was beginning to gather power.

"Some of them have bows, I can't protect all of us while we fly," she said. "Now hush, if you have any fighting magic, then I suggest you bring it to bear."

I looked towards Sir Grelor's sword where it lay on the sand and tried to reach for it with my mind. I found the hilt, and grasped it, but the object was too heavy. Riv actually saw what I was doing and shook my shoulder. "You've never done anything that big. You're all theory, Brother, wise, but not well fought. Let me be your guardian."

"I have to try," I replied, my hope waning. "There's nothing for me to use here, and I'm not an elementalist."

"Wait!" Riv said, picking up a handful of sand and showing it to me like it was a new discovery. I instinctively slapped it away. "You've thrown rocks at me plenty of times, chucked my dice around when you're keeping me from the games, why not just use sand! Whip up a storm, get it in their eyes, choke them," Riv said.

"You're right," I replied, realizing that there were piles of red hot sand less than a hundred feet away. I strained to move the surface sand with my mind. It came easily as I channelled my fear and outrage into the act of creating a wave of loose, searing sand that swept across the first line of knights. I had never felt so much power, and it grew with my confidence.

I could feel the wind resisting against the grains I pushed with my mind, and employed tricks I'd come to know to persevere, manipulating the wind inside that half of the stadium itself. The sudden exertion was beyond anything I'd experienced before, and I was covered in sweat, breathing in quick pants as I poured all my fear and hate into the act of grinding the enemy knights down.

They were so close, ten feet away from the tight ring of Draconian Guardians, when I fell to my knees. Riv regarded me with wide eyes. Over his shoulder I could see a thin smile on Rakiz's narrow face. My sandstorm ripped through the enemy knights; I could feel magical barriers against projectiles and heat starting to break down, but they were too well fortified for me to break through completely. I slowed them, I awed the Crusher Duke and the knights around me, Rakiz stepped back and observed.

That is when I found it for the first time, the spirit in the stone as some of you know it, the innate knowledge of that element in particular. They had a mage, somewhere in the rear ranks, and he tried to attack my mind directly, as though stabbing at my mind with a sharp knife, but Rakiz stopped him cold.

I reached out to the sands, could feel the hot glass forming into solid crystals, and began to exert my control over it. To anyone not schooled in the magical disciplines, it seemed as though nothing at all was happening. My sandstorm abated, and the air cleared except for a fine yellow dust. Rakiz was letting me have this fight. I can only assume she wanted me to feel the power of a combat magician for the first time in my life.

The Urgyle Knights came together rapidly. forming a shield wall. "It's over, Captain Naruna!" shouted Carmack, the Crusher Duke. "Withdraw and fight another day."

"Charge!" shouted a knight in grey tinted armour. He wore a flag pinned to one shoulder - tattered, thanks to my sandstorm. "Your eyes will clear once we've broken their lines!"

The first enemy knight charged, and I raised my arms, muscles tensed, my fists clenched. Wagon loads of sand moved, reheating and whirling along the surface of the ground, becoming a mixture of grains and liquid glass. I could feel Rakiz lend me a portion of her power as I focused my furious attack on the front line of the knights. A mental image of molten glass rising up and collapsing on them, entombing them, burning them, suffocating and crushing them filled my mind. I felt the heat from the sand melting into liquid glass on my face and I could feel one unlucky knight's boot sink into the scorching liquid. I was doing it; before any of our enemies could reach us, I would crush the first wave, and show them what an Ondi-Ne mage could do once he began to come into his power.

A familiar hand landed on my shoulder then, and I was instantly relieved when I looked up to see the face of my master, Nauso, looking down at me. "It is time for us to go, Naze."

I looked through a veil of watering eyes to see a half-wall of glass frozen between my allies and the King's knights, I really was doing it, but Nauso stopped me, something I'm grateful for to this day.

I could feel his will surround us, and we were transported far from there in an instant, leaving the mess Riv and Sir Grelor had caused well behind to resolve itself.

Chapter XV

The most powerful human elementalist wizard was named Azcro. He was the master to Coriath, the Deliverer, and it is said that he appeared several times while searching for his former apprentice. He said many things about his apprentice to the people he found who cursed his name and sung his praises.

There is one encounter I'll never forget reading. Azcro appeared in the middle of Louwer, a neighbourhood in central Brightwill that was once a village before it was engulfed by the endlessly sprawling city that crawled across the continent. He was immediately approached by a Wayist Ava-Ondi who warned that he would prevent Azcro from interfering with his township, even if it meant he had to duel him.

Azcro simply found a quiet place near the street to sit and did so. The Ava-Ondi followed him and asked him what he was doing. The wizard simply asked, "What has my apprentice done here?"

The Ava-Ondi could only reply that Coriath had visited them, but stayed for only one night and caused no harm. Upon learning that Azcro believed he was accountable for all the actions of his apprentice, the Wayist Master's attitude changed dramatically. Coriath was regarded as the most powerful human sorcerer to appear in Brightwill. During his brief time there he not only taught humanity how they could practice magic, but he demonstrated how one can be brought back to life by appealing to forces in the afterlife, thus, the use of shrines became commonplace.

He expected that humanity would be elevated intellectually once he removed some of the mystery surrounding magic, but Coriath could not have been more wrong. He only introduced another dynamic of power, and instead of bringing equality between humanity and the rest of the races, he allowed some of the most malicious tyrants to access power that was beyond their wildest dreams. They had opposition within humanity, yes, but they were not so opposed to the overthrowing of the Ava-Ondi rulers who had suppressed them for over a century. By the time humanity's quest for freedom became one of the bloodiest revolutions in our history, Coriath was long gone.

Azcro, his former master, saw the war for humanity's freedom beginning, and he witnessed the first Ava-Ondi and Ondi-Ne town burnings during the Liberation War. He saw thousands of them drowned in their own town squares. Even children who had magical talent and were not hidden in time were killed with their parents. Azcro told the Ava-Ondi what was coming, that he knew that the township of Louwer would be attacked within days.

The Ava-Ondi Wayist Master and his students would be no match for the Warlocks and their army. Azcro told him the actions of his former student, Coriath, and everything that resulted was his burden, and offered to transport them to a land far from the continent of Brightwill, where the Ava-Ondi and the Ondi-Ne that lived alongside them would be safe.

When the Warlocks led their human army into the township days later, they found only Azcro there, who told the Warlock, "In the hands of an enraged child, anything can become a weapon," before standing completely still and waiting for his response.

The Warlock saw the statement as an insult – most scholars agree that it was, even though it was fairly accurate – and attacked Azcro. The master of the Winds was unaffected by any magic, sword or arrow, and half the day was wasted as the Warlock's army tried to attack the man, who had only assailed their leader with words. When the place where he stood was burnt to ash, the woods nearby were well aflame, and the empty village nearby was ruined, Azcro only smiled wearily and asked, "Was that not exhausting?"

This lesson is chronicled in Ondi-Ne grimoires, because it teaches that the truly powerful do not need to use their own resources to perform great magical feats. Azcro was human, yes, but his magic was universal, as far as we can know. Anyone with an open mind and dedication can learn to use it, but when he performed a great feat that day in front of the Warlock, his acolytes, and his army, they were all confounded. Azcro the wizard collected all the energy they used in attacking him to restore the land, and the village was replaced by a thick forest. He took a broach from his pocket and used the remaining power he'd collected to enchant it. "You can all be wonderful people, and do great things," he said before disappearing.

Most of that army disbanded within the week, making their homes there, in a place they called Willwood, and some time later that place became legend. Three years later, for no reason anyone has been able to discern, it disappeared. The name of the Warlock who led that army has never been discovered either, but it is known that one of his acolytes was called Looth, and she went on a well known search for the last free dragons that lasted until the Cinder War.

No one ever found out what happened to Willwood, or to the Ava-Ondi and Ondi-Ne he warned about the approaching army. Azcro appeared several more times across Brightwill, and several such towns disappeared. He only saved seven out of hundreds, but it was obvious that he felt responsible for the actions of his student, Coriath. Back then, when Riv and I were in the middle of our jeopardy, Azcro was still wandering, looking for his student, but I did not find out until decades later.

As Riv and I appeared in the tunnels beneath the Woodland District, I couldn't help but think that Nauso must have felt a little like Azcro. I had almost used the foundational knowledge he taught me to commit an act of horrific violence. Even though I was guided by Rakiz into performing the act, I knew I could have stopped it from happening. I had also allied with an Ava-Ondi who betrayed her kind. Sure, all of it stemmed from my brother's actions, but I made matters so much worse.

If Nauso thought at all like Azcro, then my transgressions were his, and there was a lot to answer for. To my knowledge, he couldn't whisk us away to some far off haven, either. "I'm sorry," I said into the darkness.

"Maydo, Riv, are you two whole?" Nauso asked.

"As far as I can tell," Riv answered.

"Yes," Maydo replied. "You wouldn't happen to have something for Riv to put on?"

"Here," Nauso said. I could hear the rustle of cloth, but my eyes had not yet adjusted to the near perfect darkness.

"Thank you. Which end is up?" Riv asked.

"They're trousers," Nauso said. "One side has two holes, the other has one big one."

"How did you get us here? I felt it happen, but we moved without moving. I saw the energy weave around us, through us, but I don't understand how it worked.," I said.

Nauso illuminated the space with a ghostly yellow light floating above his head. "Several streams of energy pass directly beneath the arena. One leads to our district. I was able to steal one of the Passage Stones before I escaped from the temple. I can't keep it for long, it's from Coriath's garden monument."

"They kept you in that garden?" I asked. It was a practical garden that grew what the priests called sacred food. They sold it to people to offer at their shrines for highly inflated prices.

"Chonolo said he feared that there would be attempts on our lives. He moved everyone there; we didn't have a choice when the Guards turned up on our doorstep."

"I'm so sorry," I said. My heart was heavy with the disruption Riv and I caused.

"You should not have trusted Rakiz, that is true. But from your perspective, I understand that you didn't see any other option. If you hadn't aligned with her, I don't know that we could have gotten you both out in time. Riv, maybe, but you would have been at Rakiz's mercy. If I could have gotten a message to you, tell you that Chonolo had us sequestered, you probably would have made the same decision."

"Why did she want to do anything with you, anyway?" Riv asked.

"She's been looking for an Ondi-Ne with great potential to teach for years. There are talents that come naturally to our people that are impossible for Ava-Ondi to learn unless they are demonstrated. I suspect you were an obvious target, since she's come here asking about you and a few other students before," Nauso said. "Chonolo also wants to learn from an Ondi-Ne, so I can only assume that they're working together to learn our ways."

"I've never seen them here before," Riv replied.

"Of course you didn't," Maydo snapped. "You're as blind to what's happening around you as you are to the consequences of your actions."

"It was that knight's fault, who reacts to an insult like that?" Riv said. "He was a thin-skinned half-wit, all of this is his fault."

I was so angry that I slapped him out of reflex. It was the first time I'd struck my brother in real anger, and I hit him so hard that he was driven to one knee. My hand stung. "You idiot! Your big mouth is what caused all of this! We stay out of their way, that's the rule with humans, but you mouthed off like some foul simpleton! Now everything will change; humans will be talking about your bloody gremlin act for years! We're supposed to keep out of sight, but now you're famous!"

"I can't help what they did! Guards held me down and nearly drowned me in buckets of paint that smelled like the underside of a wallowing pig and tossed me out to get killed!"

"I'll be happy you're alive when you've learned to keep your gob shut! Until then I'll just expect more trouble, and I might not be there to save you!"

I felt the tapping of a tiny fingertip on my shoulder then. It was followed by small feet settling there, and I immediately recognized Oroza's fragrance, like recently tilled earth. "Gently, you are two of the same," he said mournfully.

"He's right, I couldn't have said it better," Nauso said. "You're two halves of the same being, born together. Neither of you should say anything but 'I'm glad you're free and alive' to each other until you calm down, perhaps not even that much. Oroza, how is the way ahead?"

"The humans have stolen our food, our bigger shiny things, and they're bringing fire," he said. Oroza couldn't help but speak like a frightened, saddened child, that's what he was then, after all. "Little humans sing around the flames."

"Then we don't have much time. We have to save the grimoires and our weapons stash," Maydo said, already starting to make her way up the tunnel. "Oroza, hide."

"I can help?" he asked.

"You can't see the grimoires, they're hidden from Dragon Kind, remember?"

"Oh," Oroza said.

"Ride under my chin, and stay out of sight," Nauso told him. "I would be heartbroken if you were ever harmed."

"I'll be careful," he said, before disappearing into Nauso's robes.

As I rushed up the tunnel behind Nauso and Maydo, I couldn't help but feel more angry at the thought of humans from Lowboard ransacking our home while our people were at the temple. My deepest rage was still reserved for my brother, who I believed was responsible for everything.

I regained focus as the smell of smoke filled my nostrils, and we neared the door hidden behind Wursa's house. We pushed up the hidden trap door in the back of her large kitchen and rushed in. I'd never seen that room empty before. She was like a mother to so many of the younger Ondi, Riv and me included. Her home was more of an inn, once built for her husband and five children – all of them gone. She made sure she was always cooking for people, that Ondi with problems finding a place to stay had a bed in her home.

That kitchen was always bustling, and we were always welcome at the long tables in her main room. I learned about herbs, tubers, and other foods from her, but most importantly, Riv and I learned about our parents. Wursa was a good friend to our mother, and spoke of her often. I never grew tired of it, but as Riv and I grew older, we visited less, helped in the kitchen less, but were happy to drop off whatever we could steal.

That's the way of adolescence; you look forward to accomplishing whatever goals you are invested in, or spend your every waking moment working towards a cause you've embraced, and you forget the people who have been helping you your entire life. At least, that's how it was with Riv and me. We were focused solely on becoming independent, and would do the worst kind of work to earn our way to that.

Much like Wursa's home, those ambitions had become hollow. I believed I did my best to save my brother, and I would do everything I could to further the cause of my people. If there was one thing my brother demonstrated to me, one important thing, it was how small the Ondi-Ne were compared to the rest of the world. We were on the verge of being crushed, forgotten, extinguished completely.

"I'm sorry, Naze," Riv said as we rushed through the empty common room in Wursa's home. It was a whisper, only for me, in a tone I'd never heard before. He was pleading. We arrived at the single window and saw the green pillar in the middle of the district in flames. The green garden planted in that vertical column of homes was ruined, along with the prospects of our people feeding themselves honestly for the next few months.

We'd have to use thievery and magic to keep food in our bellies, and if we were caught, it would give our King the excuse he needed to drown us all in a vat at his feet. Over a dozen human children danced around the flaming pillar, while older ones tore at our doorways, enlarging them so they could ransack our houses. "I'll forgive you," I said to my brother. I was still furious, but Nauso had taught me so well. A long time before then he'd told me, "The first step to forgiveness is to invite it into your life," and by telling Riv that I'd eventually get over the trouble his loud mouth caused, I was doing just that.

Besides, it was easier to hate the humans of Lowboard for what they were doing. Riv couldn't have known that would happen. Chonolo must have, though. Someone that wise would have to be aware that taking all the Ondi-Ne in, forcing them to abandon their homes by telling them danger was imminent, would leave the district open to attack from the neighbouring humans. "Chonolo did this on purpose," I said.

"Why did you leave anyway?" Riv asked Nauso.

"The city guard didn't give us any choice, Chonolo was with them, made them promise that our homes would be safe," Nauso said. "We've been relocated five times as a people in my lifetime. It only led to an improvement the first time, when the Ava-Ondi pushed us out of our first home, the Nekum, the old tree village, when it was rotting. I suppose our people are too accustomed to being moved."

"I don't see the guards now," Maydo said. "Riv, we're going to my spot under the old wall stones, you know the one."

"It's about time I get my hands on real blades," he said, grinning.

"We don't want a fight here, there must be a hundred humans running around on this side of the district, and more blood won't further our cause. I'll cause a distraction if we're spotted, you get the blades and get back to your brother. Make sure they get out with the grimoires."

"What if I get attacked?" Riv asked.

"You'll get free and run," Maydo said. "You're almost as fast as I am, I doubt any human could catch you unless you're surprised, so don't get caught unawares."

"Okay, okay, no blood," Riv said.

Maydo looked to Nauso, who nodded, then she and Riv were off. They leapt from the window, rolled across the ground, and ran along the edge of the narrow street, staying close to cover. I'll never forget how quick they seemed.

"Now for us," Nauso said. "Follow me, stay out of sight."

I'd known Nauso all my life, and had never seen him run until then. I always regarded him as an old man, though he was younger then than I am now. At a pace that kept me breathless, he led me out the window, across the alleyway, and into the cobbler's house. From there we took back doors, crossed through two gardens, and passed through two more homes that were connected inside by doors hidden behind kitchen shelves.

Before I knew it, we were in a short passageway beneath Nirda's home. She was one of the few people in the village I barely knew, a grower and collector of flowers. She sold rare pigments to humans to make her living. "This isn't where the grimoires are hidden," I said.

"These are the originals, I showed you to this passage three years ago, don't you remember?"

"I'm afraid not, maybe it got buried under my training?" I offered as he opened a wooden box to reveal the three Ondi-Ne grimoires. Their covers were normal leather bound with strapping and meticulously sewn string.

"Maybe, or you could have been distracted that day. Riv was getting into trouble around that time."

"Now I remember, I was called away because he was found with too much coin, no way he earned it," I replied, recalling the hiding place then.

"Ah, yes, pickpocketing," Nauso said as he handed me a thick leather pack. I held it open while he slipped the three grimoires inside. There was a fourth beneath that I didn't recognize, with a white cover made of moulted dragon skin. The skin itself was restored and toughened until it made for a near indestructible slip-cover with a flap that wrapped around the book seven times.

"What's this?" I asked, recognizing that it must be an important book.

"I suspect this may be one of the articles Rakiz would lust after if she knew we had it. There are several books like this in the world; the Ondi would be foolish not to write many tomes on this topic, but this one in particular is quite comprehensive." Nauso held up the book, it seemed heavy in his hands. "Shiny!" Oroza squeaked from where he rested in the folds of Nauso's robes.

"Not for you just yet, Oroza," Nauso said.

"Rats," the little dragon grumbled.

"This is the Book of Serpent Law, a veritable manual on practicing magic with the same forces dragons use when they reach their third enlightenment. I've already begun teaching you a few of the fundamentals, and Maydo has passed one of the Gathering forms to Riv, but we've been doing so without telling you that the knowledge is out of the ordinary. If there was any sort of practice that would make the other races, humans especially, nervous, it would be the kinds found in this book."

"Wait, what are the Gathering forms?" I asked, concerned that Riv could have access to magic. He was enough trouble without it.

"Nothing to worry about, especially since he hasn't mastered it. But, pay attention next time you see him practice his forms, if he does start to get the Gathering form right, you'll know right away."

"It might help to know what it is though, just in case," I pressed.

"In case of what?"

"Trouble?" I asked.

"Listen, your brother may not always manage to keep himself out of trouble like you do, but he's a fast learner, and I know he didn't mean to get any of us into this mess. He'll be endlessly regretful, and he needs someone to be on his side, to tell people that his willingness to earn forgiveness is genuine."

"I know, but he keeps getting into trouble. This is just the biggest, I can't help but think it's-"

"Not the last time he'll find trouble?" Nauso said. I could make out his smile in the dim light. "Most likely not, but I bet the next time he gets into trouble, it'll be for the right cause. This terrible mess is going to be painful for you both, more so for him, though, because he's going to blame himself. If you're there for him in your own unique way, you'll find it's enough of a learning experience for him to start thinking things through before he takes action, you'll see."

We made our way out of our district without event, joined by my brother and Maydo near the main tunnel intersecting with the sewer. "Half the Woodland District is burning," Riv said to me in a subdued tone. I could tell he was absolutely crushed; he had taken everything that had befallen our people onto his shoulders. For the first time since he shouted at that knight, I had sympathy for him. "The humans ran off, too much smoke for 'em."

"We'll make this right," I told him. It was an unplanned statement, but I believed in it just the same, not that I wouldn't remind him what his big mouth got us into, but I'd be by his side as we made up for his part of the trouble.

"No one got killed," Maydo said. "Homes can be rebuilt, people are a bit more difficult."

"Magic people ahead," warned Oroza. "Big magic."

We slowed down and chose an old, corroded sewer grate to peer through. Sure enough, there was Rakiz, a small contingent of Urgyle Knights, and the Crusher Duke. "It's fine," I said. "I can pretend to pledge myself as her apprentice and leave later. I'm sure they won't hurt anyone as long as I'm cooperating."

"No. There's no pretending when it comes to Rakiz and pledges," Nauso said. "Look at the brand just above the Crusher Duke's wrist. See that triple cross?"

I looked for a moment, waited for him to turn the right way, then saw it. There was a triple cross just above his wrist, from there I couldn't make out a few of the details, but it was definitely there. "I see it," I told Nauso.

"She's enslaved him," Maydo said. "I recognize it from the fighter pens."

"Exactly. No matter how kind he seems, he's in her thrall," Nauso said. "And with a touch of her hand, you would be her slave as well. We can't go back, the tunnels are filling with smoke, heating up. I'll have to face her."

"You won't be alone," Riv said.

"You're right, he won't be," Maydo said, "but you won't be involved. I'll support him. As soon as you and Naze see an opportunity to slip away, you go. No hesitation, understand?"

"Don't lose these," Nauso said, patting the heavy backpack on my back. "Countless Ondi have contributed to those books, including your parents."

"I won't," I told him.

Maydo reached into a black backpack my brother was wearing and withdrew two curved swords in their scabbards. They were ornate, with fine metal and cloth weave-work wrapping the hilts. She pushed her own, simpler blades and scabbards into the pack before cinching the whole bundle up tightly. "You're not my best student, but you have the most potential, Riv. You'll be on the road to mastery if you focus your will, I've already given you the tools."

"I can fight at your side, I can find focus, Master," Riv told her.

"Strength, Riv," she told him. "Focus on getting yourself and your brother to the temple, then tell them what happened here."

"Chonolo and Rakiz are working together, taking this opportunity to capture the last of the Ondi-Ne magic," Nauso said.

"Nauso already has a plan in motion to save our people, you don't have to burden yourselves with that," Maydo said. "There's no way to keep so many safe without leaving Brightwill. A few can survive, hide easily, but all our people? The King's knights will have us drowned if Rakiz doesn't take her pick and imprison us, so he has a solution. You just have to let Nauso and I get over this obstacle first, so do nothing."

"All right," Riv said.

"Nothing, I mean it," Maydo reinforced.

"I said all right!" he replied more convincingly.

Chapter XVI

I was raised in an atmosphere of war and suppression. Every day I recalled that the human king, Hosten, had my parents drowned in a vat at his feet. Before that he defeated them, tortured them, stripped them of the little jewellery and clothing they had. Every day I was keenly aware that humans made that happen as soon as they were given the power to do so. I didn't hear about the negotiations they attempted with the Ava-Ondi that ruled them before the Liberation War until much later in life. I was a child who hated humans, and opening my mind to the idea that they were very similar to Ondi-Ne in the way they thought and felt was a near impossible task for Nauso. That was a lesson he could teach, but I wasn't open to learning it. It took me years to accept that humans were so much like us, and most of them hated what the Liberation War did to the Ondi, especially the Ondi-Ne, who didn't rule over humanity at any point in time.

Still, every day I remembered what happened to my parents and who was responsible. What was worse, there was no refuge in Brightwill. Every King and Queen joined in the persecution; they had been waiting for a reason, it seemed, to unseat Ondi who held any power, and to make sure they could never rise again.

That war led to increasingly worse times, my life continued as it began, accompanied by wars separated by periods of uncomfortable peace. I would like to tell you I am one of the most enlightened beings here, that I found ways to bring wars to an end before the land and countless lives were scarred, that I avoided conflict, but I have seen combat in every war since my adolescence.

The Upheaval was the first. Where a single King was unseated, an act that inspired assassinations of the ruling class across Brightwill. The entire continent fought over who should rule for a decade. I left before the war ended, but I can tell you I was deeply involved for years.

The Order War was next, a conflict that began in the shadows between rival Mystical Orders. This I tried to prevent, but when it came to fighting, I was with the Cinder Order, and killed more than my share of Masons and Bearers. Their Orders were our chief enemies, and I allied with several humans in my order to fight for supremacy at first, then to prevent our own Order's extinction. It was for naught; the Cinder Order was defeated, disbanded, and I left Brightwill for years to find my peace.

I returned to begin work here, to build this refuge as the Cinder War began because I saw little chance of survival for anyone. Dragons from another world were eventually brought in by Charthanga and his followers. They called themselves the Cinder Order, resurrecting many of the traditions of the Order of Wizards I once belonged to, but they disregarded many of the core values that made that society great. The Dragons they brought forth were strange to everyone, impossible to control for long, unwilling to return to their home realm, and most of all, they were hungry. Charthanga had the upper hand he wanted for a short time, long enough to burn entire country sides and to feed entire armies to his dragons, but they strayed, and by the time we drove much of his dragon army back through the doorway into their realm, Brightwill was ruined. Necromancy and Pyromancy were Charthanga's specialties by then, and he had absorbed the power of several other worldly dragons, leaving their physical forms to roam the continent, mindless and ravenous.

When the Cinder War was brought to an end, not all the new dragons were destroyed, but they relented. Charthanga was defeated and dealt with, but the destruction that war brought was historic, world changing. Even though I believe I was on the right side, I cannot look across the land beyond our walls and not feel shame.

There are other wars between those large, history defining conflicts mentioned, and I'm sure there are people in this auditorium that would like to remind me of them, but we are short on time, so I'll get back to my story.

As I said earlier, even as an adolescent I was no stranger to war, or death, or killing. Even though I was the more peaceful brother, I knew I'd eventually have to kill a human, perhaps many humans. Not for revenge, but for survival. The men and women of Lowboard seemed to be encroaching at all times, the world around me seemed hostile, giant, dangerous. The Knights, the guards, and many other humans regarded Ondi as a pest race. There was no end to the danger I felt, even at home, even in my own bed, and I'd remember who killed my parents the next morning, then the cycle of fear and hate would begin again.

As we emerged from between the bars in that sewer grate, we could hear the crackling of the fires consuming our home behind us. The smell of smoke filled the air, and I had already decided that my brother wasn't the real cause of it all. It was the human plague, and the betrayer of all Ondi, Rakiz, who still looked untouched and beautiful despite what had transpired in the arena. Though her thrall, the Crusher Duke, donned his weighted gauntlets reluctantly, I expected terrible things from him if he had to join the fight. The flat bars across the knuckles of his gauntlets were polished to a shine, but I could imagine what they looked like after he'd bashed an Ondi into pulp; that was where his moniker came from, after all.

"Naze promised to become my apprentice," Rakiz said. "No one goes back on a pledge to me."

"Well?" Nauso asked me with an upraised eyebrow.

"Only if she saved Riv." I told him.

"Interesting. She didn't save you, did she Riv?"

I looked towards Riv and only then realized that Maydo wasn't standing beside him. He was grinning as he responded. "I saved myself," Riv explained with a bow. "Then Master Nauso spirited us away, but I would have found a way out for me and Naze, no doubt."

"No doubt," Nauso said with a chuckle. "So we have no business here, Rakiz."

"I expended resources, traded favours that could only be called once, and lost face with the King for your student. His apprenticeship is a small price to pay for that, and to his benefit, I might add," she replied. It was evident that her patience was growing thin.

"None of that was necessary," Nauso said. "You should have come and spoken to me first. Besides, you can claim credit for doing great harm to the Ondi, that should restore you in the eyes of our King."

"That's enough!" said Chonolo as he pushed through the front line of the King's knights. "By the authority vested in me by the Bearers and the High Temple Seat, I demand you surrender all magical paraphernalia."

"Finally, the face of all this," Nauso said. "How long have you been waiting for an opportunity to end us and take our secrets, Chonolo?"

"The ways of magic should be open to everyone! Keeping knowledge secret is an affront to the natural flow of thought and ideas," Chonolo said.

"Reciting Bearer Doctrine only makes you out for the shallow vessel you are. If the ideas I hold were meant for you, you'd have already had them. Besides, I would have enjoyed having you as a student if you came to see me. All my knowledge would be yours in time, and what you could do with that knowledge would only be limited by your mind and your race," said Nauso.

"Become the student of an Ondi Woodlander?" Chonolo scoffed. "You overestimate yourself, and the uniqueness of your people. Humans can perform any magical act the Ondi-Ne can. We are the source breed, from which all intelligent creation sprung."

I saw Maydo for an instant then, crossing between a narrow space in the street between her and the legs of the knights. She was amongst them without notice, too small, too quick to notice.

"I only wish that were true, understanding between our Orders would come more easily. Unfortunately, the secrets of creation are still a partial mystery to all but a few."

"Coriath, the realm traveller, the Vagabond and God Seer proclaimed as much! Humans are the most common race, every world he visited, he encountered but minor variations of our form, of his form."

"If we're taking the word of only one man," Nauso countered, "why not believe Parano Gardner, who stated that humans are descended from fish, the Ondi-Ne from trees, Ava-Ondi from birds, and Ondi-Un from worms. He preached his message for years longer than Coriath the Vagabond."

"Only his followers can call him that!" Chonolo retorted.

"Oh? I'm not enticed by your saviour or your Order, they seem to enjoy surrounding themselves with limitations. Ondi-Ne are but small in size and number, but we celebrate all our freedoms, including the right to invite people to become honorary tribe members. Would you like to cross this bare patch of dirt and become one of us? I offer you this, and apprenticeship without any extra provisions, and with the fullness of my forgiveness." I knew Nauso's offer was genuine, but I was also keenly aware that he was buying time.

Chonolo actually looked confused for a moment, but his expression darkened. "I wouldn't associate myself with your filthy brethren. We were willing to settle for the secrets your apprentice held, but now I demand that you surrender into my custody. I will have your grimoires, and you will demonstrate your ways at my leisure."

"Ondi-Ne do not imprison people or rule by force," Nauso replied, his expression becoming stony. "And we can only be pressed so much before we resist. I offer you one last chance at brotherhood instead of blood."

"You would threaten me?" Chonolo said.

"This is tiresome," Nauso said, sighing. He was entering a trance only a few of his students knew, myself included. To any onlooker, he would seem calm, but his trance allowed him to be in complete control of his abilities. It took him a heartbeat to enter it fully but it took me much longer.

I concentrated on relaxing and letting go of my fear, my confusion, and I was confronted with a much more daunting internal foe: weariness.

Youth is incredible, it has to be stated. If I were that weary now, I would retire to my chambers, or retreat from any opposition, given the choice, but not then. With youth as my ally, I was able to bear it and press on.

I got in touch with my inner self, the unquestioning being that I was, that wanted few things, and wanted them clearly. I wanted freedom, I wanted to find a way to remove fear from my existence, a way past anger, and even though I'm loathe to admit it even now, I wanted revenge. Trances and meditations are difficult when you're young; you find more instability, and more intense emotion. I commonly found a simmering anger when I managed to meditate deeply, and as I sank part way into my trance, that anger flared.

To the humans looking on, it seemed Nauso only took a brief moment to close his eyes, but to us it was as though we had a portion of the day to sink into calmer states. When I had finished making what was left of my power available to Nauso for whatever he was planning to do next, I opened my eyes and asked Rakiz, "Did you have anything to do with killing my parents?"

She hesitated, and then answered, "No, child, I was only saving myself those days, trying to help humanity strike a balance in the world."

"Calm, Naze," Nauso whispered. "Concentrate on assisting me. This is not a fight we can win, and she didn't know them."

I was shaking; she betrayed Ondi kind and I couldn't believe that I entertained the idea of becoming her apprentice. The whole notion seemed ridiculous, and I'd never felt more wrong. I should have known that Nauso would save Riv, that humans like Chonolo never offer to help Ondi, and that anything that came from humans was tainted, or offered with an unfair price attached.

"Sense the problem we're correcting now," Nauso said to Riv and me.

"Whatever it is you're doing," Chonolo shouted, his face turning red, "you are to cease it at once!"

"What's going on?" Riv said, his hand sliding towards one of the blades tucked into the folds of his tunic.

I felt it then, what Maydo and Nauso were trying to alleviate. "Chonolo is holding us here, Nauso can't shift us out," I muttered to Riv.

"Do your fellow temple guardians agree with the sequestering of Ondi and your plot to steal our secrets?" Nauso asked.

"We are unanimous!" Chonolo barked back. "Now stop whatever you are doing!"

"You can't sense it? My presence in your mind?" Nauso said in a placid tone. "I may have secrets from you, but you have no secrets from me. Your plans here have met a great deal of opposition. It's only a matter of time before Woodlander sympathizers put an end to your involvement in this plan and Rakiz is forced to do things her way."

"That's impossible! There is no power that can penetrate my being!"

I knew that instant that what Chonolo was saying was true. Nauso wasn't focusing on reading anyone's mind, he was holding his efforts in reserve, maintaining his focus, taking no action. "Thank you for confirming what I suspected," Nauso said with a kindly smile. "You're right, I couldn't touch your mind, but I could distress and distract you."

Maydo's knife was at Chonolo's throat then, her grinning face pressed up against his from behind. "Release your hold on us," she said.

The knights noticed her then, and drew swords. Chonolo raised his hands, focusing magical energy between them. His hands would be on Maydo next, and I expected her to suffer terribly or worse, but she was too quick. She drew her blade across his skin, cutting through most of his thick human neck. With her other hand gripping his ear, she let go of him, dropping to the stones and drawing his head back. The grisly sight will never leave me, nor will the realization that someone who helped in raising me could be so deadly if pressed. She attacked Chonolo with the intention of ending him; the blade she used was an Eilwun, an old Ondi-Ne enchanted weapon that prevented whatever destruction it did from being repaired or healed. She truly wanted Chonolo dead, and he was.

With Chonolo's will gone, Nauso was able to shift us away before Rakiz interfered. I had more time to see how that spell was woven, how the energies swept the four of us up and carried us invisibly to our destination, the Temple Gardens.

"I thought we were about to fight," Riv said, his disappointment plain.

Normally, I would object to the notion, but in that moment I realized I not only agreed with him, but I was disappointed as well. "Me too," I said. Judging from the expression on his face, I could tell you he was more than a little surprised.

Chapter XVII

I recall being stunned by the sights and smells of the Temple Garden. It was more expansive and bright than I could have imagined. It is difficult for me to believe, as I stand before you, even while I show you what I saw then in a grand illusion, that we are in the same space over a half-century later. The garden is gone, but if you use your imagination you can smell the citrus trees in bloom, the herb gardens, and even the fragrance of rare flowers.

Amidst row upon row of vibrant growth were signs that the Ondi-Ne and Ondi-Un were once the masters of the place. Little marble statues of our old gods and goddesses, great patriarchs and matriarchs, decorated the paths. Some were pretty but coy like Illa, the Mesmeriser, others chased each other playfully, a few were stoic, like the Waveway Master, Solir, who some say is still alive somewhere across the sea. Gods of plenty and goddesses of fertility peppered the garden between memorial pieces celebrating our legends, and even there we had enough statues hiding between the rows to pay appropriate tribute to the tricksters, who some say are some of our most important gods, goddesses, and ancestors. I remember thinking on how the humans who took over stewardship let the statues become stained and chipped, another slight they made against us. The Ondi never defaced their shrines or statues of worship, it simply didn't cross our minds. I realized much later that the condition of our garden statues was most likely not declining because of any malicious act, but through time and neglect, something that afflicted shrines and monuments from all races and belief systems eventually.

The marble tiles beneath my feet were unyielding and slippery, but I was anxious to see my people. I had never been so nervous in my life, I was afraid they'd hold me accountable for what had transpired, along with my brother. I could feel a powerful barrier surrounding the garden, no non-Ondi-Ne or non-dragon could enter, so I didn't fret our casual pace.

Oroza's little head popped up from under Nauso's collar as we walked down the garden path, between giant stalks of cane and rare ferns. "Something's wrong," he said, poking Nauso in the cheek.

"Nothing's wrong, everyone's in the middle of the garden," Nauso replied. "And we're just in a hurry, that's all."

"No, with you. You're sad. Not the kind of sad that comes when I've stolen biscuits or eggs, but the kind of sad when someone's dead or dying."

Oroza could be oversensitive. He wasn't a confident creature back then, but what adolescent is? I was used to ignoring some of his overreactions, but I suspected that he was right that time. "Is there something wrong, Master?" I asked.

"Ah, there she is," he said, ignoring me completely.

We rounded a corner and entered a clearing with polished blue and black marble tiles. A woman sat on a bench crafted in the shape of a great stag laying on its belly. She was a tall human with long raven hair. Her robes were simple, though she laboured under a shawl of tiny coins finely chained together that jangled and tinkled as she moved. Despite her advanced age, I could see that she was still beautiful, and that it could only be one person – The Nidela – a wanderer sorceress who turned to peace during the onset of the Liberation War then disappeared. I remembered her from my childhood; her visits were always a matter to excite our parents, and she always had these wonderful toffee treats that kept us chewing away in a corner for hours. I realize now that giving children such time-consuming treats is really a way to keep them out from underfoot for extended periods of time, but we didn't care then, and that's the beauty of the trick.

All I remembered about The Nidela other than her treats back then was that she was searching for something that had all the Ondi-Ne adults interested. I hadn't seen her since before my parents were taken from us, so I had forgotten her until I saw her on that bench.

"Hello Nauso," she said, her voice still surprisingly youthful. "Maydo, it's a relief to see you. I thought you had left."

"I was planning to," Maydo answered. "I couldn't bring myself to go when the time came."

"It's a good thing, too," The Nidela said before turning towards Riv and me. "You two have grown so much since I last saw you, it truly is amazing. I see great power for your Naze, and for Riv, you will create a significant place for yourself in history. I feel these prescient dreams are true, without question."

"Thank you?" Riv answered. "I'll just be happy when I see that I haven't brought on a second culling."

I elbowed Riv in the ribs and shot him a scolding glance.

"They are all here," The Nidela said, and the next time I blinked, it was true. The clearing and garden boxes surrounding it were choked with the people from the Woodland District. They carried little, some looked frightened, others regarded Riv and me with obvious disappointment or distaste, but the rest seemed eager, especially the few who were around our age. "The elders have gathered the votes," The Nidela said. "I must begin preparations, there isn't much time."

"We're going," said Essella, one of the eldest women in our district. She had a green mane of hair that always reminded me of a lion's because of its shape. "Only a few, nine of us, disagree, so we're leaving this place, and I hope leaving Brightwill finally."

"Leaving?" I found myself asking without thinking.

"Yes, you've made this place unliveable, Naze, you and your brother. Between Rakiz, the Crusher Duke, and the Prince looking to remove the last of the Ondi for his father to prove that he's truly human, this place is impossible for us."

"Easy, Essella," Maydo said, "If Riv and Naze weren't the catalysts, it would have been something else. It's obvious that the humans on both sides of this persecution have been looking for an excuse for a while."

"Don't blame Naze, either," Riv said, irate. "I made the comment that set that knight off, he shouldn't have heard it at all. None of it makes sense to me, but he did, and I killed him. I did it in defence, and I'd do it again."

"Even though it put us in this position?" sputtered Gori, an especially broad-faced Ondi-Ne, I remember him turning red from jowls to forehead as he heard Riv's words. "You wouldn't sacrifice yourself if it meant peace for us? If it meant we could stay in the land of our forefathers?"

"This land hasn't resembled the forest our forbearers knew for generations," interrupted Khaeli, a thin, grey-eyed woman who always treated us well. She was one of the newest to join the ranks of elders, and a practitioner of great magic. "This is overdue, we've only been waiting for someone to show us the way."

"And we've found it," Liva Naul said as she stepped out from behind a planter thick with thorny rose bushes. Her broad brimmed hat was gone, but her orange and yellow hair had been set free in wild cascading curls. She flashed a devilish smile at Riv and nodded. "Saw you in the arena, quick thinking, quicker feet, made for a cracking good show."

"Didn't work out in the end," Riv said, still surprised by the appearance of a young woman he would have traded the sun and moons for.

She was only two years older than us, but next to her and the experiences I imagined she had while she was travelling, I felt like I was still just a boy from the Woodland District.

"We're nowhere near the end, luv," she said. "I've been across the Westwhile Sea, and can tell you there are wild woods there these Brightwill Kings don't dare try to tame. The Nidela wiggled her fingers, got her rings singing, and summoned me back. She knew I'd find the Far Wood, the Devouring Green, and the Yuran River when I left, but she also told me I'd be back, and here I am today, to guide most of you there. Wish it were all of you, truly."

"So the vote did not go the way I expected," Nauso said to the elders.

"You're coming with us, Nauso," Khaeli said. "I'm sorry. You're the real architect behind our escape, you brought the people we need together and set it in motion years ago. Everyone who has trained under you, worked alongside you, knows that no one else is as capable in these matters, so you will conduct the core spell. We also voted on the punishment, and came to a reasonable conclusion."

"What's going on?" Riv asked, snapping out of the stunned state Liva's appearance inflicted on him. "What punishment?"

"I'm sorry, this all had to happen quickly. Rakiz and her people can only be blocked out of the garden for so long," Nauso said. "These decisions had to be made while Maydo and I were taking care of you two."

"Riv and Naze will not come with us. Instead, you will serve an important purpose," Khaeli announced,

"You're going to make a problem, aren't you?" Oroza asked. "A problem for my brothers."

I knew he meant Riv and me. He was born the same year, we grew up in the same nursery, and were parented the same, with Nauso and a few other people, like Maydo, taking over our upbringing after our parents were murdered. "I'm sorry, Oroza," Nauso said, "You'll never know how much it pains me, but we have to take a portal to the coast to get away from the trouble here." I'd never seen Nauso weep until then, and it was one of the most haunting things I'd witnessed in my youth. There is something about seeing the man who stands as the stable pillar in your life begin to unravel that changes your world. My world was collapsing, but Oroza must have felt even worse.

"No," Oroza said, shaking his head and tucking as much of himself under Nauso's chin as he could. It was something he did when he was a tiny hatchling, curl up into a tiny ball and snooze in the warmth against Nauso's neck, resting on his collar. "You can't leave me alone," he huffed and choked as tears began to roll down his grey-blue cheeks. "I'm your boy."

"I know, you are, you're my precious boy," Nauso said, holding Oroza to his cheek. "But only The Nidela and her Coven have the power to create a portal to the coast, and I have to help them finish the work."

"Why? Why can't you train someone else?" Oroza wailed. I was sure the whole temple heard him. "Stay here, they need you too!" he pointed at Riv and me with his small hand.

"It would take months, and no one I know can feel the pathways as I do. You'll join us soon after, don't worry. Riv and Naze will follow."

"Um, why can't he go through the portal?" Riv asked me in the lowest of whispers.

"Dragons can't-" I started answering.

Oroza finished for me, his tone turning the response into an accusation against Nauso. "Dragon kind can't use human magic at all, not even for portals. You knew!" Oroza turned on Nauso. "This whole plan was hatched knowing I couldn't follow, you want to get rid of me!" He leapt out of Nauso's arms and his wings, usually safely tucked in so humans couldn't by chance see that they weren't clipped, extended and flapped until he landed on Riv's shoulder. "I don't want to go with you if I'm a burden anyway!"

"You are a blessing," Nauso told him. "I'll miss you more than I'd miss an arm or a leg, but they can't direct this portal without me. You're strong, and I've taught you everything you need to survive, Oroza, because I knew this day could come. Between the three of you I know you'll prosper."

"It's selfish," Oroza said, leaning so far off Riv's shoulder towards Nauso that I thought they'd both fall over. "You're being selfish."

Nauso stepped towards Oroza and cupped his little chin in his hand. "You know I would take you if I could," he told him. "I don't want to leave you, or your brothers, but they're right. We have no chance of survival in Ankon as a people, but the three of you can sneak away easily, even from the middle of the temple. I'll see you before you know it, because you'll get to the coast, and I'll leave a message there for you that

130

you won't be able to miss. You'll know where to go from there, and we'll be together again."

Oroza hopped from Riv to Nauso and wrapped himself around his adopted father's neck. The pair remained thusly for what seemed a long time, but no one would dare interrupt. "I love you, boy," Nauso said finally, and the little dragon leaned back so they were eye to eye.

"I'll make sure nothing happens to them for you," said Oroza through tears. "But I'm going to gag Riv."

"We'll be together again soon," Nauso said.

"I know," Oroza said. He made a flapping hop to my shoulder then, and wiped his tears away.

"It's time," said a human child with coins jangling in her braids as she emerged from a section of tall ferns. I assumed she was one of The Nidela's Coven, I could see the power she was channelling as plainly as the clothing she was wearing. Signs of human magic were difficult to view. Unlike the sorcery I knew, the weave of elemental power seemed nonsensical, a shifting jumble of colour with no spiritual sound. "We need you to join the paths."

"I'll be there momentarily," Nauso said. I didn't understand what she meant by 'join the paths' and I wanted to ask, but he was rushing on, speaking with haste.

The young coven member, I never learned her name, walked to me then, and pulled several leather thong necklaces from a bag. I caught a whiff of something foul when she put it on me. "This is a rat-foot charm, it'll keep anyone from tracking you with magic. You'll get your head start."

I looked closer and realized that the smell must be coming from a tiny bag tied in the middle of the necklace. "Thank you," I told her as she moved on to give one to Riv then tied a ribbon version to Oroza's neck. "Just wondering, is there a similar type of charm I can make that doesn't use dead things? Just in case this one gets worn out or lost?"

"It took us all day to make these three, they'll last as long as you'll need them," she said with an understanding smile.

"Naze, I'm going to leave you with one of the grimoires, The Key," Nauso told me hurriedly as he withdrew the other books from the backpack while it was on my back. "You read it tonight when you're safe, as fast as you can. Rest when you're finished, but start over again as soon as you've eaten, as soon as you can. You have the capacity to understand what's within very quickly, and the discipline to start practicing the specific talents you need to develop." He stopped and looked me in the eye with a seriousness I'd never seen before. "You'll be powerful, but don't underestimate the value of experience. Everyone you face will have more of that than you do, and that will make any confrontation very dangerous. Talk your way out of bad situations whenever you can. Humans aren't as slow as you think they are, and they're kinder than you'd expect. Remember that most humans are almost as poor as we are, that's worth something."

I found it strange and difficult to accept that Nauso's last instructions to me would include a challenge to stop hating humans, to expect better of them, but it's a lesson I am still learning to this day. "Make sure Oroza doesn't overeat after sundown," he said, glancing at his adopted dragon. "He gets bloated and has trouble sleeping."

"I heard that," Oroza croaked, struggling through a fresh onrush of tears.

"Soon, we'll be together again soon," Nauso told Oroza. "Be my strong boy."

While I was accepting instruction from Nauso, Riv was practically cornered between Maydo and Liva. "Keep your mind clear, and think before you speak," Maydo told him. "The best way to avoid trouble is to see it coming. I'll see you within the year. Keep to discipline, speed, strength, and wit most of all."

Liva had a different set of instructions for him. "It's the Prince they'll try to please now. If they don't think they can get Ondi-Ne magic out of you, then they'll try to take credit for wiping us all out, something the King and his Prince would reward handsomely. The best way to ruin that plan is to stay alive," she told him as Maydo joined the rest of the Ondi-Ne, who were getting ready for their journey. "It's the only thing that makes sense judging from the news I've been hearing from the ships passing over. The Brightwill Kings are a point of fascination for everyone on the coast and even some ways beyond. We're all watching that Prince and his father, most are sure his dad's been smothered months back. That makes matters worse for us. The Nidela has had a vision that confirms what every Ondi fears: Prince Tabbin has the Enduring Light, a source of power that he currently underestimates, but The Nidela has foreseen that this setback will push Rakiz to show the Prince its potential, and he'll become Emperor not long after. He may be one quarter Ava-Ondi, but he hates the Ondi, and will bring about a final cleansing. All Ondi will be destroyed, the Dragons will be pressed out of existence as well, not just culled and imprisoned.

"The Nidela won't let me go after the Enduring Light, but she said nothing about you and Naze. Take it, save us, and I'll be waiting for you on a friendlier shore." She kissed him passionately then. When the stare-inducing gesture was over, she pointed down a path and said, "Remember where we'd hide after stealing carrots?"

"That's our way out of here," Riv replied, a grin spreading across his face.

"Exactly. You always were quick-witted," she told him. "Friendly shores will be waiting, don't tarry."

I wished there was more time for farewells then, but I could feel the barrier holding Rakiz and her people away breaking down. A few farewell embraces were given by people we'd grown up with, people who served as surrogate parents, but after scant moments, our people were gone in the blink of an eye.

I never saw them again.

Chapter XVIII

Ondi-Ne are a difficult race to eradicate. We are resilient, resourceful, quick, and most of all, small. I don't know exactly how Riv felt, but he and Oroza were my only attachments to my old life, so I did my best to shut what just happened out of my mind and focus on improving our dire circumstances. I behaved as though he and I were the only Ondi-Ne left in the Kingdom of Rasson, and that Oroza was the only free dragon. It wasn't true, but it may as well have been if you considered my outlook.

The escape route Liva pointed out to Riv was perfect for us; no human could fit through most of those irrigation drains, and we were out of the temple before we saw any indication that Rakiz or Chonolo returned there. They were surprisingly clean, with the exception of a pair of dead birds.

There's something a lot of humans don't realize about Ondi-Ne, and it's been to our benefit since our races met a millennium ago. We experience time differently. Most humans are only a third as quick as Ondi-Ne, because they are so much larger, because they come from a land where great size was of greater benefit than great speed. If a human were to suddenly see time as we do, a nine hour night would seem to drag on for twenty-seven hours. We only sleep for three to five human hours at a time, so we are a race of all phases. We are awake during sunlight and moonlight, can sleep in the full light of noon and the utter darkness of a moonless midnight, though there are exceptions. As a result, we see better than most in both shades of light, and our vision rarely fails us until we grow to be very old. There's still a little part of me that believes Ondi-Ne are descended from the forest faeries of old, while our human counterparts come from the giant apes we used to bait and trick, if you believe in that sort of thing.

Humans seem to speak slowly and in low tones to us, that is why so many Ondi erroneously assumed they were slow-witted. That assumption has cost us dearly throughout history, especially since they adopted disciplines and magic that made time flow exactly the same for them, a set of skills that are very rare, but when a human who experiences the world as we do challenges us, well, the Crusher Duke demonstrated the kind of slaughter that can follow. His victories during the Liberation War against the Ava-Ondi armies, which many Ondi-Ne were enlisted in, detail how effective a fast, powerful human can be.

Our advantages in speed were critical as we moved through the city then. Evening was hours away, and green paint still stained Riv's face and hair. We were relegated to the alleyways, the undersides of merchant carts, and any other cover we could find as we made our way back to districts near our scorched home.

We knew of several places we could possibly hide, but they were all near the Woodland District. We turned a corner down a long alley and all three of us caught sight of something we were not prepared for: a column of black smoke rising into the sky. Our district was burning in earnest, and that meant that Lowboard, the worst human slum, was most likely also on fire. "Serves Lowboarders right, looting us and setting fires," Riv said.

"If I were an older dragon, I'd help things along," Oroza muttered.

"Our people got out safe," I said. "I hope theirs do too. Living rough is bad enough, especially in the Capital."

"You're too kind to them," Riv said.

"Goblin!" shouted someone behind us excitedly.

We whirled to face the grinning blonde Dwarf boy, who seemed so excited that I took three steps back, and a group of other young Dwarves. "No, he's a tanner, he fell into a vat," Oroza explained.

I tucked his head down into my tunic. "Too late," Oroza groaned regretfully. He was right.

"By the Reaver, that's a dragon!" said the youngest looking Dwarf of the bunch. He was even shorter than me.

"Shut your gob, Tinner," grumbled the oldest of the group, the only one with a beard and the look of a full grown adult. "We've got to get these folks to cover before you squawk on." He stepped forward, pounded his chest, then bowed to Riv. "I'm Irhiro, ninth to the name, and there's someone who's been looking for you, goblin boy."

"There are a lot of people looking for us," Riv replied. "We'll be on our way."

"If you want to survive in the Capital, you'll come with me and meet my lord. He wants to see the crown kept from Prince Tobbin's head as much as you do."

"We just have to go, get out of the kingdom and..." Riv hesitated. "Go farther, until we're away from this trouble."

"Temple guards," whispered one of the youths surrounding Irhiro, pointing towards the main street.

"No time, little ones," Irhiro said, closing the distance between him and me much faster than I'd expect from a stocky Dwarf. He wrapped his cloak around Riv and I then rushed us into a doorway. "You're a sorcerer, Ondi-Ne," he told me as we waited in the shadows. "Get a sense of me using your power, read my intentions, you can do that at least."

I followed his instructions. It was a simple enough trick, but it required calm, and I was having a little difficulty finding peace at the moment. I tried to let my mind go blank as I watched the alleyway through the slim slit in the heavy cloak our dwarven host had us wrapped in. I could tell my brother was tensing up, Oroza was grinding his teeth.

The young Dwarves, ranging from the ages of children to older adolescents, were blocking the narrow stair we'd descended, and made a nuisance of themselves by trying to sell unremarkable stones to the city guards as they passed. They were loud, insistent, and obnoxious, but incredibly effective as a distraction.

As the momentary danger passed, I was able to find enough clarity to get a sense of the situation. I gasped as I felt the void of my missing people. I had never truly sensed how much they occupied the spiritual world until they were absent. I focused on Irhiro, and realized several things. First of all, she was mother to three of the children in the alley. My assumption that her beard marked her as a man was fully erroneous, and I faintly recalled hearing that some female Dwarves of status grew long, beautiful beards. I had to admit, the feeling of it on my cheek as she held us in her cloak was quite nice, very soft.

I also realized that she represented one of the Chieftains of the Draconian Guardians, and I followed that realization as far as my intuition could take me. The Draconian Guardians were steadfastly against King Hosten and Prince Tobbin. If there was anyone who could protect us, it would be them, and Irhiro was furious at seeing the Woodland District burn. She had old memories of Nauso, good ones. Her house, old and great, had helped the Ondi-Ne move from our old district when I was still a child, and they had helped us improve the homes we found in the district that was burning as I stood there. They distanced themselves after that, on the advice of Maydo; most of our allies did. Years later, I discovered that she did our friends a great service by having them step back from their involvement with us. Combined, they would only reveal themselves as an inferior force compared to King Hosten's armies and allies. Scattered, our friends could step forward in extraordinary circumstances. "We go with them," I told Riv just as I could feel him getting ready to break free.

"Are you sure?" he asked. "It took you an awful long time to come to that conclusion!"

"Absolutely." I checked on Oroza and realized he was already snoring faintly. "I think he is too."

So, we went with Irhiro, who had us in the Stone Ship District by nightfall. That's where I realized one more important factor that makes Ondi-Ne very difficult to dispose of. We are generally very well liked by most non-humans.

Chapter XIX

I don't know when it happened exactly, but, even though we were terribly on edge, even though we'd had the worst shock of our lives, Riv and I were lulled into a deep sleep. My dread-filled dreams gave way to the chirping of birds and the fragrance of fresh bread.

The serenity was almost enough to tempt me to dig deeper into the soft, warm bed and slip back into a deep sleep, then I realized exactly how alien my experience was. Riv and I slept on beds made of rough feathers and scrap cloth for most of our lives, you had to fight just to get them flattened. Our room was cramped and we could hear the other orphan and homeless Ondi-Ne around us. I couldn't hear the sounds of morning there at all, let alone the delicate sounds of dawn birds chirping. This wasn't home; that had burned to stone and ash. Wherever I was, I was sure it was strange to me, new, and unsafe.

I opened my eyes and sat up, quickly taking in my surroundings. Scanning the room, I could see there were two human-sized beds and three smaller cots. There was no stove in the room, and a large trunk in one corner sat open, empty. There were many nooks and shelves that were empty except for a huge chamber pot, a washing basin, a few cups and two decanters filled with water.

One human-sized bed was a mess, as though children had been wrestling in the sheets, and I had slept in the other, seemingly alone. My things were piled at the foot of the bed, and I wasted no time in checking them. The grimoire was there, along with a new leather bag that would easily fit into my pack. I opened it to find a tight tube of parchment, a pair of well made blank books, and an Amberquill in a walnut wood case – a fortune in craft tools for me, things I could never afford and wouldn't risk stealing. Beneath my bag were Riv's weapons, safely rolled up and tied in their leather case. We'd had no time to gather other things from our homes, so there really was nothing else to discover except for my half worn-through shoes.

Just as I was about to begin worrying about the next terrifying fact, that I was completely alone in an obviously human home, I heard someone coming up the steps. I reached out with my mind and managed to lift a sheet off of one of the small beds. It drifted across the room and stopped to hover over the door under my direction. With a good night's sleep, and after the experiences of the day before, I found the task much easier to perform than before.

The door swung open to reveal Gronin the Knight. Out of his armour, he looked almost as stocky and powerful. He was carrying a broad tray burdened with bread, milk, cheese, steaming bowls, and cool ones brimming with fruit. "Ho! He's up! The new Prime Magus of the Ondi-Ne!" Gronin announced with a grin. "Already wielding some kind of magic, judging from those hands of his, gripping the air. Stay your hand, great wizard, I pray thee."

Riv was following close behind, grinning, and I concluded that we were most likely safe, at least for the moment. "You should see the *food* they have here!" Riv said as I directed the blanket to drop onto him instead of Gronin. He would have dodged it if I wasn't forcing it down at speed. "Hey!" he protested as he struggled out from under it and bundled the blanket up. "You're getting better," he said as he tossed the bundle at me.

Gronin placed the big tray on an end table and dragged it to the foot of my bed. We were able to sit on the edge of the bed as we ate from the tray, where we found a big bowl of pre-shelled hard boiled eggs. I believe it was that scent that caught the attention of Oroza, whose head emerged from the crumpled blankets of the other human-sized bed with urgency, his eyes wide. "Eggs?"

I breathed a sigh of relief. Everyone I needed to account for was in the same room. It was a strange room, but I could see Oroza and Riv at the same time. That was a good start atop a great rest.

"My sister took you here instead of our family Hold," Gronin said, picking up an egg and gently lobbing it towards Oroza, who eagerly caught it in his mouth, which could open wide like that of a baby bird. "I have cousins and brothers who are dead against any Ondi-Ne crossing the threshold. Didn't matter that I reminded them that Stone Shapers built the bones of our home. Most of the lords and Ladies in my house have a deep love of the Ondi-Ne, going so far back you're in our oldest records, especially during peace times. They'll turn the rest of my house in your favour, but they're off taking care of business across Brightwill. Seems we survived the Liberation War only to enter into an endless merchant's war, one of the reasons I went looking for an old order of knights who would take me. Anyhow, we were able to find the next best place for you, the Charming Corsair. Know where that is?"

I had no idea, I'd never heard of the place, I didn't even know what a corsair was, but it sounded like a bar or inn. I watched Riv as he took his place at one end of the tray and pulled a large slice of honeydew melon from a plate. "I haven't the foggiest," I said. Riv passed me an apple slice the size of my hand.

"Take a look, lad, it's a view you won't soon forget," Gronin said, dragging a stool to the open window.

I took a bite of the apple. It was sweet and juicy, nothing like the crabapples I'd become accustomed to. I walked to the window, then climbed up on the stool so I could see. I couldn't help but make sure Gronin wasn't within reach of me - I was going to be in front of an open window at a potentially deadly height, after all. He was stepping back to the tray so he could pick up another egg for Oroza, who was on the edge of the opposite bed. "Best game in the history of games, this is," said the dragon before opening wide again.

Gronin wasn't kidding about the view; it really was breath taking. When the Capital, Ankon, was at it's height in that day, there were whole districts built on bridges criss-crossing older sections of the city, and we had been carried to a tavern atop one of those high streets. I could only determine that we were near the docks on Lake Owber, a few hundred feet above the markets there. I got down lower to the sill so I could inch over it just a little, and see the edge. At street level, there were haulers drawing baskets of cloth, food, stone, and even people up from the city below.

Looking towards the Lake, a forest of masts and sails waved in the wind across a long coast of wood and stone docks. Birds wheeled in the air above, between columns of smoke rising from trade and industry buildings crowding the streets of the trade district there. We were at least a couple of hours from our home district. I looked to my left and saw another raised district, perched on a broad curving bridge. The homes and businesses seemed to grip onto the edge, leaning out as far as they could to maximize their piece of sky. A sudden wave of vertigo struck and I pushed back from the sill. "That's Gammon Street Over Chyme," I said. It was a street Riv and I had learned to ignore, perhaps an hour's walk from the Woodland District.

"So that makes this?"

"Scomer Street Over…" I trailed off. I simply didn't know. I never really cared about the distant streets in the sky, and never expected to visit one in my lifetime. Wealthy people lived there, people with old money. The only time those people mattered to us folk below was when they dropped something particularly large or heavy over the side.

"You're already close," Gronin said, throwing Oroza another egg, which the young dragon had to shuffle sideways to catch. He chewed the flesh, filling his cheeks and rolling his eyes in pleasure. "Never fed a dragon before, I'll have to tell the Hold Kitchens to keep a fair number of eggs on hand just in case one drops by," he said to no one in particular. "We're on the street they call Mosin Over Carrinaw, only a stone's throw from the King's palace. My uncle owns this inn, he's a great sympathizer of the Ondi-Ne, fought alongside them during the last war. Did you know the Draconian Guardians were on your side as well?"

"No, I thought all the knights that weren't fighting us turned away," Riv said before I could get a word in. My stomach grumbled, and I decided eating my apple slice was more important than prodding the conversation on.

"The Draconian Guardians did pretend to turn away, but some of us were allowed to support you in secret. My uncle left entirely, fought in the open. I wish I was so brave, but it wouldn't have changed the outcome. Even still, I ran supplies, supported you in a few skirmishes, but I was young. Think I met your father once, good man, he was, great commander of sorcery and a dangerous wizard."

"He wasn't a fighter," I said through half a mouthful of apple.

"Oh! He was at the end, when he knew that his fate was sealed, fighting or no. Commanded the charge on the King's palace. Your mother was no different. Didn't meet her, but she was a shadow walker, a ripper. They still tell children about the rippers, how they came out of the shadows and tore human flesh from bone with their very will. Not far from the truth."

"She would do no such thing," I retorted, quietly, but my anger at the allegations must have been obvious.

"I tell you they did," Gronin said, much of the good humour draining from his manner. "She was a healer, known for it, admired for it, but in the end, when the King marked them and thousands of your kind for drowning, for slaying, both your parents turned their good gifts to war, and they killed the hundreds, maybe the thousands they had to. They were protecting you two, and your entire people, all the Ondi-Ne left in this city were fighting for survival, and for him," he pointed to Oroza, whose mouth closed, and eyes bulged at the story Gronin told.

"They fuse a dragon's wings with Coriath's magic, and bind their power with old words from another place. Another place where it's said that there are no Ondi at all, no Dwarves or living shades or sky flame or quick amber or children of shale. But humans have had magic for many an age. The inner circles of human lords and magicians know very well that Coriath wasn't the only one who brought their kind of magic into the world, and many of them were violent travellers who would teach darker talents for a price. That's the kind of magic they use to make dragons low, useless beasts that can only dream of flight, of grasping the power of the universe again. At least some dragons are allowed to live. Your parents both had the dreams, the visions. Nightmare prophecies of a world wrecked, burning and broken because of the new human power and the near eradication of Ondi, that includes us Dwarves. They say Ondi-Ne came from the forests, Ava-Ondi from the sky, and Ondi-Un from mountain stones. Those Ondi-Un are us, they're Dwarves, and your parents could see a day when you could fit all of us in one place, and the last dragons slumber deep in the earth, trying to sleep through the age of humanity. Your parents fought like devils when they had no other choice; they killed hundreds of humans, and if you ask any human who isn't so poor that they don't know where their next meal is coming from, they'll tell you they've heard of them. They'll tell you they don't even believe that they were drowned in the presence of the King, that they were so powerful that they could return some day."

"What?" Riv asked.

"It's nonsense, but there are humans, like Chonolo's followers, who believe that the prayers at the temple shrines may bring back the wrong thing, like your parents, and that they'll be more powerful than ever. No Ondi has ever returned, so there's no chance there, I'm sorry, but it's a fear some humans have, and they stay away from shrines. The rest, the ones who know that you can't control what comes through those shrine portals, either leave the Temple or stand guard, allowing people to keep sacrificing and praying at those shrines because the money's too good to stop them.

"Back to the point I was making. There were greater warriors than you parents, those you probably heard of, but they're gone as well, even Nauso and Maydo, who had to live with the shame of hiding while people like your parents were sacrificing themselves, trying to win the Liberation War. I think Nauso and Maydo were heroes just as much as anyone who fought, hiding the innocent. Bringing them up so they can fend for themselves is more important than drawing a sword, or bringing magic to bear. I feel the sting of their absence, our cause is weaker for it."

"They had to go, they had to protect our people," Riv said, surprising me. I thought that if anyone would be bitter, it would be him, but there was no trace of it.

"I'll never forgive them for leaving you here to protect Oroza alone," Gronin said. "There's no getting you to the coast, either. Not for months, maybe not for years. Prince Tobbin has paid all the Kings between here and there to put their men on watch, and he's posted a bounty. Nine gold dragons, coins as wide as my hand." He held his hand up; it was calloused and broad, but most importantly, wider and thicker than a human's. If they made coins that size out of gold, they would weigh as much as any Ondi could carry with both hands, perhaps more. "If Carmack didn't slip me a message, telling me to keep you safe, you'd already be in their hands."

"The Crusher Duke sent you?" I asked, alarmed. I immediately rushed to my bag and started packing. "We're going," I told Riv.

"But!" Oroza blurted, disappointed. "Eggs!"

"Hold, Mage Naze," Gronin said. "You don't have to worry, he doesn't know that we're here, and thanks to those charms, there's no way for you to be tracked. Carmack may be under the control of Rakiz, but she can only command him. Between those commands, he can do little things, like signal me to watch you and Riv. You'll be moving on to another place soon, somewhere I don't know about, just in case Rakiz suspects something, and commands Carmack to tell her everything he knows about your whereabouts. He'd have to tell her about his signalling me."

"Then we should move quickly," I told him.

"I agree, but not before you've had a breakfast," Gronin said. "You look like little stick-men, you should fill your bellies while you can."

"Aye, he's got the right idea," Riv said.

I was outnumbered, and had no choice but to join in on the meal with relish. I was a few drinks of milk and several bites of egg into breakfast when a thought struck. "Say, Gronin," I asked the knight, who was leaning back in a chair sipping from a cup of thick, hot tea.

"Aye, young Magus."

"What do you think would happen if I offered something like the Enduring Light at a shrine? Something that powerful…"

"You've the thinking of a wizard, no doubt," Gronin replied, his gaze turning skyward. "You'll have a chance to ask an expert. I hear you'll be moved to a place where you can learn a thing or two about human magic. I can only assume there will be a master of some kind there. Don't tell me anything else about this plan you're cooking, just let it simmer 'til you meet someone that can help."

I nodded, my mind working through the possibilities as I finished breakfast. Gronin seemed trustworthy, but going along with his plan meant that we'd be hiding on terms dictated by him and his friends. I didn't know any of them, Riv didn't know any of them, and Oroza couldn't afford to trust anyone over three feet tall.

As soon as Gronin left the room, Riv was at the keyhole, watching him go. This was clear language; he had something important to say and didn't want to be overheard. I started eating faster, digging a hunk of bread from the heart of a small broken loaf and taking a large mouthful of egg before tossing another towards Oroza, who caught it with both hands and nibbled at the top. He was getting full. "How do you feel about going our own way? We don't know anyone who's offering to help, someone's going to turn on us eventually." he muttered.

"Maybe not today, tomorrow, but eventually," I agreed. "We have a better chance on our own."

"It's the only way to be sure that we stay free," Riv whispered, joining me at the tray. "We'll be more careful this time, find a better hiding place, like Grunn Hollow or something."

"How do you feel?" I asked.

"Going our own way was my idea," Riv replied. "I've not changed my mind since, it's only been ten heartbeats."

"I was asking Oroza," I said.

"Oh, right," Riv replied before chomping into a big apple slice.

"Not many Draconian Guardians left," Oroza said, shaking his head. "If they took us into their keep and the knights protected us, it would be safe for a while, but then, war." It was true, hiding a dragon, even one as small as Oroza, was difficult. Human knights outside of the Draconian Guardians would eventually discover that they were hiding a dragon, and then they wouldn't rest until Oroza was pacified. The Draconian Guardians wouldn't surrender him willingly, so there would be war, and they would be wiped out, being one of the smallest circles of knights. Oroza continued. "We can hide where no one can reach. Then we can steal the Enduring Light and get your parents back. Kill the Prince and his father, too."

Riv and I stared at him, open mouthed, shocked. He spoke of treason, high acts of magic, and murder in such a matter-of-fact manner that we were stunned. I couldn't deny thinking about all those things, but without Nauso, I didn't feel like I had any guidance in such grand plans, and until that moment it was stuck in my head that we should make for the coast as fast as we could, a journey that would take months if we were lucky.

"I want to find the dragons," Oroza said. "They keep them in a special dungeon, and I'll never see them while the King and his offspring still live."

"All right, but I need time. I have to read the grimoire, I need to study intently, quickly. Master Nauso wouldn't tell me to do it if it weren't important."

"Don't worry, we're at the top of the sewer system, and all the aqueducts run along these streets. Hiding is going to be easy," Riv said. "Maydo made sure I at least looked at how these high streets and the aqueducts were built, said they'd save my life one day. I thought it was boring, always tried to get away from those lessons, but now..." He shook his head. "I should have listened. I think I know enough to get us away, though. We just have to pick our moment to escape properly. Gronin is carrying two purses, you notice?"

"I hadn't, no," I replied. My mind was still reeling at the very idea of committing regicide. It didn't seem possible, to start, and it was astounding that something like that was on Oroza's mind. Understanding his thinking would come a little later, after I began to realize how Oroza longed to meet other dragons. The rarity of his species was a sadness he carried with him always, even at that age.

146

"Well, if he's carrying two purses, he's either too rich, or one of them is for us. I'll take one from him, that'll be the signal for us to escape."

"Be careful, we don't know this area well."

"Don't worry, you stick to sorcery and being all preoccupied with the complicated stuff, Oroza and I will do what we're best at."

"I do not get preoccupied," I replied. Oroza and Riv both snickered. "It's called studying, contemplating." They were only more amused at my protests. "As you like. I'll take care of the higher thinking."

Chapter XX

Without warning, Naze's knees buckled, and he dropped to the top of the dais. His head was swimming, and he realized that, over the past hour, he had become more conscious of the illusion he was projecting than where he was. The unfettered power of the Enduring Light was elevating his ability to manipulate the world around him to heights he'd never suspected possible. Doril was at his side before Naze was entirely aware of what was going on, and his hands on his shoulders invited an experience he did not mean to have with his old friend. He allowed the man to feel what he was feeling, and to see the entire scope of what he was about to do.

Doril gasped and fell to the marble top of the dais beside him, sitting down hard. "That's more power than anything in creation should have," Doril said, "and an act that every magical college has forbidden since the dawn of time."

"It is the only way," Naze said, focusing on the moment, trying to see through the haze of power brought on by the Enduring Light. "Brightwill burns, and the rest of this world is tinder."

"I saw it," Doril said, "I know, I just can't believe it can be seen, all the possibilities of the future leading to one thing – the complete breaking of our world. I've never imagined anything so damning."

Naze's head finally cleared enough for him to realize that there were people from the auditorium seats below coming to offer aid. He carefully stood and raised his hand in a gesture for them to stay. "I'm all right. My knees decided it was time to take a nap, it happens with old, overworked joints."

"Take a rest, master!" cried someone.

"That's an excellent idea, make sure that one gets an extra plum at dinner!" Naze shouted, to the mirth of many. The air around his hand focused, gathered, and an instant later, there was a firm, ripe plum in his palm. That, he did not mean to do, but there it was, fully formed. He lobbed it roughly in the direction of the suggestion to the astonishment of the younger members of the crowd.

"That one, there," Lizabe said to Kovak, directing him to pick up a fine, padded, backless seat and bring it to Naze. She took a moment to go to Naze's side. "Some of your magic goes wild. I've been keeping it with us at the top, but the weave has been noticed by several instructors."

"Are you sure?" asked Doril.

"If I can see it, they can see it," Kovak said. "When you told us what your masterwork would be, I didn't grasp the enormity of it."

"Oh, and I tried to tell him," Lizabe added.

"Aye," Kovak agreed.

"Do you want me to stop?" Naze asked. The question was foolish; stopping would mean the end of him, and now he knew, life on the world he'd come to love so well would end within the next century if he didn't finish his task.

"No. Every time I see Oroza, I wish for healing that no one has the power to give. I know the risks," Kovak said, looking to Lizabe.

"Neither of us would stop you," she added.

"Master! What's going on?" asked a voice from the front row. There was no respect in how Urgines used Naze's title. He started to stand and climb the stairs, gathering his blue and white robes.

"He's going to finish his lesson in time for dinner, don't worry, Tutor Urgines," Lizabe said.

"I'm asking what's going on, what's the intention here?" he asked.

"He's not going to be convinced by the truth, and I don't want to lie to him," Naze said as he sat and smiled at the rest of the group gathered.

"While virtually everyone here has lost much in their lives, he's profited."

"She knows him, she knows his story," Kovak reassured Naze and Doril, who stood beside his master's seat. "Don't worry."

"This is a presentation that uses illusion and it will culminate in an act that will benefit everyone here," Lizabe said. "You can trust in that."

"Trust is a valuable commodity, and one few earn from me," Urgines said. "I see magic and power weaving a complicated web above you, and I won't be manipulated without knowing the intention!"

"So you have no trust for Master Naze or anyone up here. Do you think he'd save you only to manipulate or harm you?" Lizabe asked.

"He would not!" cried Sylvest, the only Ondi-Lon in the refuge, and perhaps one of the last to exist. He'd chosen to be male, as the Ondi-Lon had to do in polite society, even though he could be mistaken for either sex depending on the day or his mood. "Naze has had a hand in saving everyone here, Urgines, and you have no right to question him. Your confusion at the master's puzzle is not cause for your disruption. Can't you see he's weary? Can't you see that he must complete his action here regardless?"

"That's all good and fine, but I won't be an object of manipulation!" Urgines said.

Naze watched Lizabe's big blue eyes scan the crowd for a silent moment before she spoke again. "If anyone else objects, please stand and make your plea."

There was some discussion between masters, and tutors, and elder students, and even wild practitioners. All of it was quiet, and Naze could plainly see some of the more talented members of the audience were explaining their interpretation of the whirling weave of power,only visible to the trained practitioner, to others.

This was the moment Naze feared. There were people out there that knew what was going on, what he was up to, and how the next few moments played out depended on how they explained what they saw, and how everyone took the news.

Urgines' eyes went wide after he spoke to one such group of elders at the front. "You seek to manipulate time?" he howled at the dais. "That is forbidden by your own law! Reality itself will be changed on a broad scale, because everyone knows the Great Naze doesn't do anything small, does he?"

"Yes," Naze said. "This must be done. I've located a moment in my life that will lead everyone down a better path if it were changed. That is why I'm telling you this story, so I can be sure of the moment I choose to change, and you can all know why that moment is so important. I have brought the wars that scarred and ruined the greatest civilization, and the largest unified continent of our history. I am responsible for the destruction of Brightwill and the coming fire that will sweep across the world. The paths that were made into other realities, to other realms, were closed by people like us, so we thought, but we have only barred the doors. It is only a matter of time before those doors are broken down, and a new horde of dragons along with things we have not beheld yet will invade, and there are not enough of us to defend Brightwill. They will come, they will see the wealth that remains in magical power, they will find a way to take it and leave Brightwill, then our entire world, barren. They will take the survivors too, slaves to humankind, dragonkind, and to beings we can only strain to understand. In my haste to prevent this once during the Cinder War and times before it, I didn't consider that there would be too few of us to maintain the barriers we erected, too few to rejuvenate Brightwill once the wars were over. The doom we face is of my making."

There were cries of denial and dissent from the audience. This was something they didn't want to believe; they loved Master Naze, and it made his heart glad while it caused his guilt to grow. No cry was louder or more contrary than that of Urgines. "You are not a god! No singular being is so important. You can't cause decades of war and strife, or bring about a world apocalypse!"

"I have!" Naze said, his voice striking the audience like a shockwave. The power within him was becoming more difficult to control, but he took a breath and pulled it together around him like a blazing shroud. "I allowed my brother to become the villain our people blame for the destruction we've witnessed in Brightwill when I was the one who became the reaver, the travelling assassin, and finally one of the lords you feel when you reach too far into the darkness. I am the standing dead, my body trapped in time in the last moment before my natural death, in violation of even more of the laws I expect my people to follow. I am the one who once hunted necromancers and became the greatest of them. Charthanga learned how to be a powerful war magus because of his contests with me. He was able to summon the Sky Reavers, those unfamiliar dragons that hail from other realms, because I left enough of a crack for him to wedge into and pry wide. The Cinder War would never have happened if I hadn't gone on my early quests for power. Even my efforts to bring us all together here, to create a refuge, is motivated by selfishness. No one wants to be alone at the end of the world; I was hoping to recreate a village, like the one I knew as a boy."

"Grandstanding," Urgines said. "Meaningless grandstanding!"

"Go," Naze said, his voice booming across the auditorium. "Anyone who does not want to see this done firsthand should leave. Be aware that there is no way to stop it without prematurely tearing a hole in this reality. I am connected to realms that are in the midst of creation's maelstrom. The three portals trapped inside the Enduring Light will no longer be balanced if I am stopped now, and they will erupt, opening to raw power of a scale none could control."

"You grasp at things no one can manage, and you will fail, die, then leave us to suffer," Urgines said. "And no, I won't watch it."

"Your intention is to change events somehow, to lead us to a better situation?" asked Eliani, a grey-haired Ondi-Ne who was nearly twice Naze's age. Her voice was strong, but her tone gentle.

"That is my exact intention. I wish to explain myself, to remind myself of the events first," Naze said.

"I understand, and I stand by you, Master Naze," she said. Eliani looked to the people around her then. "I remember the time Naze speaks of, and I was in the Kingdom of Zeshe, closer to the Eastern shore. I have no doubt that the story he tells is connected to the disasters so many of us have known. While I have doubt that he was the cause, I do know that events surrounding Prince Tobbin and his father eventually led to my people crossing the sea, and going into hiding. The power our people had in Brightwill, though small, was entirely gone for decades thanks to those events. People who guarded important secrets for generations were forced to flee, and those things were unearthed by others who had impure intentions. If the change he brings alters that, then there will be more of us, wars may be averted. Brightwill may have a chance, and I hope it does, because I can tell you, so much of it was still beautiful when I was younger. I long for it even now. I defer to your wisdom, master."

"You saved her from a Quick Amber slave camp," Urgines said. "Of course she's on your side, of course you have her blind trust."

"Weren't you leaving?" Lizabe asked with an upraised eyebrow. "Farewell, Tutor Urgines."

"Mark my protest!" he shouted as he strode down the aisle. When he reached one of the arches at the end, he looked back for a moment. "He's wondering why no one goes with him," Kovak said with a snicker. "No one else here is as wealthy as he."

"Or values those coins more than the possibility of a better world," Lizabe said.

"That was, perhaps, the last chance I have to stop," Naze said. "Are you still with me, old friend?" he asked Doril. The man didn't know that magic was the only thing keeping Naze on his feet, that he was truly extending the last moment before death, and had been for years.

"I'm with you," he said, sitting down beside him and taking his hand. "Tell your story."

Chapter XXI

I never turned on Riv. I never looked at him and told him that his trouble with knights, getting the attention of people we had no business dealing with, or the departure of our people was his fault. Well, not after the first time I made the accusation, anyhow. Of all the arguments my brother and I had from that point on, that was not one, and I've thanked my lucky stars more times than I could count since I lost him that that argument in particular never happened.

I knew he felt guilty, so did I. He may have gotten us into trouble initially, but my rash choices made things much worse. Accepting Rakiz, allowing myself to be led around while he was in danger, those things were my fault. I had a powerful master in Nauso, and could have refused any help save his, made sure I got to see him in the temple when Chonolo forced our people to go there. I should have run directly to the Woodland District when the trouble started, but no, I took the hand that was offered first. In the end, there was plenty of blame to go around, I'd have decades to consider which burden belonged to who, and even concluded that the matriarchs and patriarchs amongst my own people were also to blame. If they didn't trust Chonolo and the Temple guard, if they were not so accustomed to being pushed from one home to another, if they were not so passive, things would have been very different. To this day, I believe that there would be thousands of Ondi-Ne here, not a few hundred.

We can only hope that with time and experience comes wisdom, and with wisdom comes a more intelligent perspective. Looking back at the situation and everything that happened only brings me to one conclusion: our circumstances in that time created the perfect conditions for our enemies to exploit us, then to remove us, and they took their opportunity the moment it presented itself.

We were a people of refugees, and had been moved from several districts to a few, then from a few to one, and finally to the Woodland District. Years ago, I realized that the wisdom of Nauso was absolutely valid. As much as I would rather have seen our people fight in those days, go underground, I can't expect leaders like Nauso and Maydo to subject all their people to that kind of struggle. In his place, I would have done the same. I would have regrets, but I would have the satisfaction of knowing that I saved as many as I could. Was it the right decision, in hindsight? Perhaps not. I still don't know where they went; I have not been able to sense them in all the years since I bid them farewell in the garden. I have searched, and Oroza sacrificed his ability to fly thanks to his efforts.

I can only hope that they found a place where they could flourish in peace.

I didn't have any of the wisdom I do now when we were in that inn room. All I had was guilt and frustration. No, it was beyond frustration. I had anger. I kept it all in check, but just barely. The idea of escaping from Gronin and his friends was appealing then, because I had seen what happened when other people take the initiative and moved Ondi-Ne for what we were told was our own good.

It brought us to that room, where no hope felt genuine. I know Riv felt the same, and as for Oroza, well, he resented humanity more than anyone here could possibly comprehend.

We packed in haste, not sure when Gronin would return. All things of use in that room were squirrelled away, and we'd even made another pack by folding two small blankets. We packed linens and feathers from the mattress so we could create a bed somewhere else. In that bundle, we shoved the nuts, uncut fruit, bread, and any other food we could manage. Oroza took refuge in my backpack, while the rough-fashioned one was tied to Riv. "No worries about falling backwards," he said. "It's like wearing an overgrown pillow."

"Well, our dinner's in there somewhere, so try not to fall at all," I reminded him.

The sounds of boots coming towards our door silenced us, and we took our positions on either side of the doorway. "You sure we should run?" Oroza said from under the flap holding my pack closed. "I don't know if I trust Gronin, but maybe we should see if he has more eggs, first?"

"We're sure, now shush," I told him.

"I'll steal you some eggs and a pot to boil them in," Riv muttered.

The door opened, and my brother sprung up, slapping Gronin as hard as he could and laughing shrilly. That was the distraction. While the one hand was slapping the unsuspecting Dwarf, the other was pulling Gronin's coin purse free from his belt. Riv didn't stop there, though. To my shock and amusement, he leapt atop the poor knight, riding his shoulders with Gronin's face buried between his legs, bucking and thrusting as he shouted, "All hail the Dwarf Kings! All hail the rulers of the mountain! Dig me a hole! Find me a Dwarf! Toss him in! Follow him! To the gems! To the gold!"

I took the opportunity to pull loose the looped knot holding Gronin's other coin purse to his belt, then I ran through the door with the heavy bag of coins in hand.

"What in all the-" Gronin shouted, shocked but amused just the same. Before he could push Riv off, my brother vaulted off the Dwarf's head, flipped, and landed beside me in the hall, behind Gronin. We were down the stairs and out into the street before the poor Dwarf realized we'd liberated his coin.

We ducked into an alley where well-dressed, astoundingly clean people were in line with jugs at a fountain. A statue of a comely maiden with broad hips perpetually poured water into a large basin where clear water gathered. "The aqueduct must be nearby," Riv said.

I reached out with my mind, tried to see beyond my normal sight, and found the path of stone for the second time. The first was when I was

156

able to take control of the sand, this time I could feel the way the stones lay under my feet and beyond. A few of the humans there actually smiled at the sight of us. The children in particular seemed thrilled to see Ondi running by.

I was glad we were moving past, and we wouldn't have to find out if their attitude would change once the surprise subsided. "This way!" I shouted, redoubling my efforts at speed.

"Bumpy back here!" Oroza complained. "Going to sick up!"

"Not on the book!" I replied. "Lean out of the bag if you must."

"Too many..." He was interrupted by a backpack shaking belch. "Eggs," he finished mournfully.

The entrance I saw in my mind came into view as we turned down a blind alley. It was a small wooden door leading under a grand house's crawlspace. We were in and through in moments, from the bright light of day to the absolute darkness beneath someone's home. We waited for our vision to adjust. I felt Oroza leave the backpack, take a couple of steps, then heard him heave. The stench of egg vomit filled the small space. "Bloody hell," Riv said, coughing.

"By Hyra-Ondi's grace…" I said, covering my mouth and nose.

Oroza belched and sighed. "Better."

"Can't hide down here much longer or I'll be adding to that pile," Riv choked.

"Don't worry, there's a hatch," I said, pulling a small Quick Amber bulb from my pocket. The magical fluid inside illuminated the space with a soft yellow light as I shook it slightly. An old metal hatch was just a few feet away. It took both Riv and me to open it. We were able to stick a thick sliver of wood in to keep it open. Inside, we saw exactly what I pictured in my mind: a slow moving stream of perfectly clear water with a broad stone walkway to either side.

I made sure the pack on my back was sealed tight and leapt down. The shock of cool water made me gasp for air as I resurfaced. Oroza was right behind, avoiding the water by gliding in a tight circle. He carried Riv's bundle, a few feathers drifting through an opening to be carried down the dark channel. Riv was last; the trap door slammed behind him as he took the wood sliver holding it open.

We were on the walkway a few moments later. "This water is crystal, cleaner than anything I've seen," Riv said, slurping a double handful into his mouth.

"This is the heart of the Capital's aqueduct system," I replied. "The water comes from Mount Speri, comes through these high streets, then goes down to most of the districts."

"Never got to the Woodland District," Riv said.

"No, never got that far," I agreed.

"Any humans down here, you think?" Riv asked.

I closed my eyes and tried to reconnect to the stones around us. All things have a memory, especially stone. The more I opened my mind to reading that memory, the easier it became, and after a few moments of relative silence, I could hear it. The stone whispers to those who are close to that element, and it told me of such a history. That is, until I was surprised by the sound of Riv urinating into the aqueduct! My eyes snapped open and I told him, "Humans don't come down here until there's a problem with the water! They might check on things if someone complains that it tastes like piss!"

"Too late," Riv said. "Bad luck to stop a flow once it goes." He finished as I shook my head, and as he was closing his pants back up he noticed the laces of Gronin's money pouch hanging out of my sagging pocket. "You got him, too?" he asked, surprised.

"Aye, first time I've lifted a purse," I admitted, grinning. I would never admit it then, but it was liberating, exciting to break a common law to our benefit.

"I can't believe it!" He laughed. "I'm proud, my brother of many disciplines."

"You left him with nothing!" Oroza said, cackling and rolling on his back. "He'll probably have to clean pots to work off whatever he owes for our room! And the food!"

Riv found that exceptionally funny, and though I couldn't help but smirk, I was eager to move on. "There are places where no one looks, the older section of the aqueduct. The rest gets patrolled when the workers feel like checking for obstructions, but not often. Hard to tell when they come down."

"How'd you find that out?" Riv asked.

"I listened to the stone," I told him as I tightened my pack. The absence of Oroza made the backpack sit uncomfortably.

"Fine, don't tell me," Riv said with a shrug. "Lead the way."

After a relatively short walk, we came to a side passage that was blocked off by bars. "The old section of the aqueduct system. Humans never come here." I told Riv as I slipped through the bars.

"No doubt, it's less than four feet high," Riv replied. "Perfect for us, and it's dry?"

"The water was diverted a long time ago."

We made our home there for two months or more, the exact duration is foggy, because time was not a great concern then. I can still remember every corner and angle of our makeshift home, and I can still hear the gentle flow of the water around the corner. Throughout the sprawling, closed aqueduct, there were hatches that led into the wealthy homes and shops of the High Streets. Though it made me nervous, Riv went on plenty of excursions late at night, returning with food that I never dreamt of. He once emerged from a service door that led directly into a wealthy kitchen.

The cook was busy at her oven, and to Riv's surprise, the old woman gave him a cranberry apple pie, patted him on the head, telling him, "Oh, David, you must learn to stay out of the kitchen, you'll become fat in my company!" She turned him around and sent him out of her kitchen. That pie was one of the best things I'd ever tasted, and I told Riv he should revisit that kitchen, but something about the mistaken identity and the senile old woman kept him away.

I took Nauso's advice, and read through the grimoire he'd given me. It was the key to understanding Ondi-Ne magic, surely, and what I learned over the ensuing weeks while I read the book over and over, taking notes, doing exercises, would form the foundation of everything I know. I communed with stone before I slept, tracing paths throughout the city above and below. That was the true beginning of my love affair with history, and with the language of my chosen element.

Riv practiced with his knives, listened to humans the few times they passed by the bars around the corner, and diced with Oroza for the first week. After that, he continued to practice, but Oroza had begun to moult, and he slept more and more until he emerged with a fresh coat of scales.

The dragon skin left behind was not like that of a normal lizard. It could be soaked, and worked, and Oroza knew how it was done. The stuff was valuable, rare, and during our fourth week there, he made it into a rough pair of shoes. My brother, already an agile master of knives, had his soft, durable treads.

By the end of the fourth week, I had traced a route into the palace, and I was convinced that I wanted the Enduring Light. I could feel that powerful object, and I could feel the footsteps of the Prince on his rich tiles, ignorant of it. The stones told a simple tale, of a King who never set foot on the palace floors, and a Prince that visited the room of Rakiz for lessons in the afternoon, and something else late at night, when he thought the rest of the palace was asleep.

I had Riv begin bringing me components from the avenues above us, nothing anyone would truly miss. A few things he bought by pretending he was a child because they were locked in shops that were warded by spells that would alert the owners to the presence of thieves. One owner was happy to play along, the proprietor of High Kind, a shop for sorcerers that was four storey's high and only nine feet wide. Jhode, a wizard himself who had inherited the shop from his father, warned Riv not to visit other stores, the Tier Of Note especially, because he would be found out in an instant.

To my surprise, Jhode provided Riv with everything I requested for a more than fair price. I couldn't help but feel that we may have found an ally. Those ingredients were crucial to my learning, and I managed to create tools for Riv, enchantments for myself, and to practice several spells that would prove critical in combat, some of which I continued to use for decades. Jhode, on the other hand, had found an eager buyer in me that was interested in articles and ingredients that human magic didn't require often, if at all. He was happy to get a fair price for wares that were becoming more ornamental than useful in his shop.

I also learned a great deal about the Crusher Duke's tattoos, his brands, and was able to guess with some accuracy how Rakiz trapped him. Those markings that protected him, made him stronger and faster than a human normally could be, were accumulated through a great deal of travelling and trading. I supposed he must have sought out Rakiz for a brand she was proficient in making, and after paying her, she branded him with a control sigil instead of what he'd requested.

During the seventh week, when Oroza was so stir-crazy he wished he was moulting again, I finished a map that led us directly into the palace, and I decided that we were ready. Riv never argued when it came to that decision. He wanted to start the journey that would reunite us with our people as much as I did, but we both hated King Hosten and his son, the Prince. We also wanted to take the Enduring Light, and find out what I could do with that in my hands. Could we use it to quicken our journey to the coast? To find and free the dragons King Hosten held in his hidden dungeons? Perhaps we could even bring our parents back, or gain an advantage over the human families who ruled over us. The more I studied, the more I realized that I would have to have the Enduring Light in my hands before I knew.

Chapter XXII

The tunnels around the palace proper had more bars, and there were magical wards painted on the ceiling here and there. All I'd done for nearly two months was study and practice magic from that grimoire. Reading it through took an evening, taking in its lessons took years, but I focused on manipulating the minds of my enemies, directly transforming elements, and on the circumvention of difficult obstacles during those early days. The pair of books Gronin or his sister provided for me were filled with notes, and then I filled two more. I'd never been a better student, and my mind has never been more excited, filled past the brim with new ideas.

"Do you think Gronin got your messages? Is he coming?" Riv asked as he checked the interior pockets of his jacket. We were on our way to the palace; if there was anything missing, it was already too late, but I knew he had what he needed. The jacket was an interesting thing though, a testament to how good Riv was at finding trustworthy people, and how quickly he could make friends. By the end of our stay in the High Streets, he knew two tailors, a butcher, several people to dice with, whom he lost his share of the coin to in the first five weeks, three kitchens that would sell to him, a grocer, and then there was Jhode.

I suspected that at least one of his new friends would betray us, but it never came to pass, and I knew Riv wouldn't share our plans with them either, so even if soldiers were ransacking our new home while we were travelling the tunnels, it didn't matter. We wouldn't be going back there.

"I'm sure Gronin got my message," I told him. "No Dwarf could miss so many directions."

"But you didn't tell him how he could respond, or where we were," Oroza said from where he flapped just ahead of us, watching for wizard wards that could alert someone to our approach. They were rare in the outer tunnels.

What I didn't know about Gronin and my messages was that he took them very seriously, and watched for them religiously, especially after the first one. I could sense only roughly where he was, and that he was alone when I delivered the messages. His friends would tell me later that the first appeared in the bottom of a stone stein. He was having a gulp while waiting for another mug to fill at the tap in his family stronghold's cellar. I admit my first attempt at communicating with him didn't go as well as it could have. He got to the bottom of his mug and found my messenger, a darkling beetle. He sputtered, coughed, and nearly choked, dropping the stone mug. "We're sorry we robbed you," the beetle told him in a squeaky voice. Even though he had seen his share of magic, he was still astounded. A talking insect was new to him.

Gronin closed the tap of the keg he was using and shook his head. "That one might have gone off," he muttered, keeping his eye on the beetle all the while.

It went on, "We'll still need your help. I hope you can gather experienced warriors to come to our aid. There will be another message."

The darkling beetle scampered off, and Gronin decided that night was not one for drinking, at least not to excess. The second message was delivered a week later, as he sat on the loo. Another darkling beetle ran in front of his feet and sang, "I'm hoping you got my first message,"

In the days since that message, he'd consulted with the High Magus of his House, Obon Teleri, who told him that it was very likely that the first beetle wasn't an hallucination, so he knew to pay more attention to the second one. I didn't hear his response at the time, but he replied, "Blimey, I did and it's not one I'll soon forget. All's forgiven, lad."

The beetle continued in its eerie sing-song voice. "We'll need five warriors who are against the Prince. I've found no trace of the King, and suspect he's dead. The Prince hides it and I don't know why."

"I'll tell you why, because he knows the people won't accept him," Gronin said, as I would discover later. The beetle couldn't convey anything he said back to me. "He looks too much like an Ava-Ondi, and the highborn know the King kept a slave consort for years. They also suspect she was killed after giving birth to that whoreson." He was unceremoniously interrupted as the beetle seemed to lose interest, then leapt up between his legs and down the toilet hole. "There's got to be a better way to get me a message."

While I was actually becoming quite talented at controlling insects that called the low places home, I sought to challenge myself. The next time I sent Gronin a message, it was though a small carving on the mantle in his quarters, which were fit for a lord of low station. The smiling dragon, on his mantle for luck, grated to life, waving and dancing. "Hey, over here!" I was listening in my way, and could sense his footsteps on the tile floor. He was listening.

"Now that's the kind of messenger a wizard uses," he said, as I'd discover later. "You're growing powerful."

"My mastery of stone increases, I may not have to use insects any longer."

"Thank grace and decency for that," Gronin said. "Now, hurry, I'm expecting a lady with a fine blonde beard."

"My preparations go well, Riv and I are honing our talents in hopes that you've found trustworthy people. I sense that you go here and there, between many districts, and I hope there are many sympathizers, people who disapprove of the Prince. I'll only send you one more message with the details of our meeting. If you're siding with us, then I owe you my thanks. If you are not, and these messages are serving as a way to gain information you will use to betray us, then I will only warn you this one time." The small dragon statue fixed him with a dire gaze. "No knightly training or magic will save you if we are betrayed."

Once Gronin realized that his smiling luck dragon statuette was frozen in that dread-inducing expression, he turned it towards the wall. I had no idea it had stuck that way, and thought it would return to its original shape. Some years later, I fixed it.

The last time I sent a message, it arrived while poor Gronin was in the bath. A stone carving of a young dwarven women with ample curves looked up from her cupped hands, which served as the faucet for the bath, and smiled at him.

"Well, your taste in messengers is getting better, I'll say that," Gronin said. "I'm getting the impression that you can't hear a damn thing I say though, you little sewer rat."

"This is the last message I can send. There are too many preparations to make, and I have to finish mastering a few tricks before we make our assault. Bring no more than six quiet fighting companions to the Unden Street Crossing, where you'll find a grate beneath the stair of a tap room nearby. There will be no moon that night. We will greet you beneath the stair when the barmaid announces last call."

"Aye, just keep this statue looking pleasant when you leave her, she pours my baths, you wee bastard," Gronin said, knowing the message wasn't getting through, especially since he'd called me a sewer rat and got no response.

A forlorn expression came over the statue then, "I warn you one more time. If your intention is to betray us, you will be in for a shock."

"Oh, no, it's going to be stuck like-" he started to say.

At the time I sent the message, Oroza was practicing some of the magic that we'd found in the grimoire that was well suited to him. More specifically, he was trying a levitation spell that went awry, and he struck the ceiling hard. "Oroza! Are you all right?" The statue turned in shock to imitate my act, asked the same question, and was forever locked in an expression of urgent dismay.

"Oi! How am I going to explain that?" Gronin shouted at the statue, just as amused as he was annoyed.

I was inwardly overjoyed when I heard the sounds of Gronin and his fellows on the way to the palace. The tunnels near the grand cistern carried sound as though the noise took on a life all its own, echoing eerily between the still water and vaulted ceilings. "I think this is the sound of them trying to be quiet," Riv said. "Are these people really going to sneak in with us? I like Gronin, he's probably a great warrior, but this isn't some brawl in the street."

"We need him, something's coming," I said.

"Rakiz knows our plan," Oroza said from where he drifted along. His wings weren't strong enough to keep him aloft while moving ahead slowly, so he used his new talent for levitation to assist him.

"You think Gronin betrayed us?" Riv asked.

"I don't think he did, I don't think he had to," Oroza said. "I can feel rage. Maybe Chonolo was more important to her than we thought; her anger is mixed with grief, and I think it's kept her looking for us. Looking for us so much that she must have found that we'd come here eventually. She's powerful, she's probably more intelligent than all of us."

I could see that Oroza was working himself into a panic. It was something that happened often enough back then, and I took a lesson from Nauso in how to put a stop to it. "Calm, Oroza. I'm here, and we've prepared escape plans just in case, remember?"

"Escape? From her and that monstrosity the Crusher Duke?" he spouted in a harsh whisper. "Unlikely." It wasn't the endorsement I would have liked, but his cynical retort did distract him from his oncoming panic attack.

"Riv, it's time," I told him.

He nodded and broke a small stick that I'd inscribed with small words of power and enchanted. In that instant he disappeared, the only evidence of him was his shadow. We rounded the corner and were greeted by three smiling Draconian Guardians. Gronin was standing in the middle, with heavily muscled Dwarves to either side of him.

His dragon bone armour was covered, and all of his knives, his swords, and other potentially noisy objects were similarly muted with pieces of black cloth. "Young sorcerer, I'm here despite your reluctance to share your exact plans," he said. "As are several of my best friends and companions."

"I'm grateful," I replied. "I'm sorry I couldn't share my plan with you in advance. I'm sure you understand."

"Aye," said a young dwarven voice. A much younger man, around my age, stepped out from behind Gronin and his knights. His beard was close cropped then, he wore a black robe cinched at the waist that marked him as a Wayist martial practitioner. He was a little thinner, and not nearly as wise as the man I know today. "Name's Kovak, and you may have my uncle convinced that you know how to crack into the palace, but I'm far from believing. How are we getting in there? Is it wise to bring a drakeling along?"

"I'm a dragonling, and almost too old to be called that, if you must know," Oroza replied, his eyes narrowing to slits.

I took a moment to explore the four men's intentions with my senses while the pair of them glared at each other and found that, while Kovak and one of Gronin's knights were as yet unsure of the situation, they had no ill intentions towards us.

"Do we meet muster, young wizard?" Gronin asked, perhaps the only one who guessed at what I was doing.

"I think so," I said, glancing at Kovak.

"My master has been studying, conjuring, practicing, and crafting the tools we need for this for weeks," Oroza said to Kovak. "Why, I've learned more than I could tell you just by being the eyes on his shoulder."

It was the first time Oroza called me master, and I admit to a surge of happiness at the thought. Confidence came with it, and the exhausting time I spent preparing was forgotten. "We are as shadow," Riv said as the knight on Gronin's left whirled to check behind him.

Riv appeared in front of him, grinning. "These ones are a little slow."

The knight raised his knife. It was caught in Riv's two tined claw, a blade catcher that he practiced with to the point of annoyance. His other hand tapped a thin blade on the plating of the knight's thigh. "A martial Wayist with blades," the knight said, withdrawing and sheathing his knife. "Very good, you'll match Kovak there. He doesn't need knives, though. He breaks bones."

Riv slipped his blades back into their proper places and nodded. The respectful acknowledgement of his skill satisfied his pride, and the young knight he'd just insulted didn't seem irritated in the least. It was a situation I was surprised wasn't spoiled by my brother.

"He's Nurn," Gronin said, patting the one Riv had faced on the shoulder. "That's Vuller, she's a rank beneath me, my second," he said, pointing at the other. "And Kovak's introduced himself. My nephew, and one of the most promising Wayists we've ever seen in the stronghold. I kept my company to the people I could trust without question, and they side with your people, Naze."

"Thank you," I said. "Now, as for our plan, it begins with ward silencing, which Oroza and I can do."

"You can see wizard wards?" Nurn asked. "How?"

"I can read stone, and make it changeable," I said, perhaps a little too confidently. I admit, I was nearly boasting. "The stone tells me where most of those wards have been scribed. The rest are plainly seen by dragons."

"We've already started, silenced several for practice days ago," Oroza added. "Had to, otherwise we wouldn't make it to the palace in time."

"You really have been at this for a while," Vuller said, "Gronin told me so, but I didn't realize how long."

"It's been a long while," Riv groaned.

"You too? I wait for wizards all the time, with their constant study, while I practice forms, then it's 'hurry along now! We must fight!' all of a sudden," Kovak said.

"When they're ready they want us to hurry up, but when we're ready they want us to wait," Nurn agreed.

"So, we go as shadow? How did you find this magic?" Gronin asked.

"It's not uncommon Ondi-Ne artefact magic," I said as I handed two shadow rods to each of the newcomers. The rods were no longer than a joint of Gronin's thumb, and he struggled to make out the inscription.

"So this is what does it, and I don't need to know a thing about magic to make it work?"

"Nope, you just break it to hide all but your shadow," Riv explained. "Then throw the pieces away to become visible again."

"Thieves' miracle tool," Kovak said as he took his. "Ondi-Ne magic, very different."

"You don't know the half," Oroza said proudly.

"You'll all be able to see me as I guide you into the palace. Do not drop these early, I only made enough for each of us to have two, and don't go too near anyone. Certain people will be able to sense us."

"Certain people? Like who?" asked Kovak.

"People who are looking for something amiss, or magically proficient people. I wonder, have you trained to fight in darkness, Kovak?"

"Yes, of course," he replied.

"Then someone like you, definitely," I told him. "So don't get too close to people."

"I've memorized the way to the Prince's inner sanctum. I'm after a little-known object made by an Ava-Ondi and Coriath. Once we have that, you can do whatever you like to the Prince."

"You don't want to kill him yourself?" Vuller asked. "Your people have suffered under him and his father."

"I'd like to see him exposed, to be honest," I replied. "I would love to see the other Kings descend on the Risen Moon Province and divide it up amongst themselves. They'll make him suffer simply because he is their enemy."

"Speak for yourself," Riv said. "I want his throat slit."

"Agreed," Oroza added. "But I want him to tell me where he keeps the dragons first."

"That's why I'm here," Nurn said, "I remember the dragon who helped me craft my armour. He's somewhere in that Prince's keeping now."

"First, how do you know the way through the palace?" Kovak asked, "It's not as though you've seen the inside."

"But I have," I replied, "It is a stone palace, and it can tell me everything I need to know."

"We'll see about that," Kovak replied. "But I'm with you. I've no love for this King, and I want to see this Prince die tonight. He had my father burned alive for arresting his magistrate. The man was harassing people on our property, my father was in the right, but still he burned while the magistrate swanned off, free."

"Funny how he died in his sleep nine months later," Gronin said.

"Then we go. We only have just enough of the evening left to finish our task," I told the group.

"Hold, how are we getting out once we've spilled blood, especially if alarms are raised?" Gronin asked.

"We're jumping out the window," Oroza said pleasantly.

"That would be a dragonling's answer," Kovak said. "What about the rest of us?"

"Naze and I can lower you down," Oroza said, "I don't just levitate myself, you know."

Chapter XXIII

With Oroza's help, I didn't miss a single ward, and they were countered before we passed by them. Whoever put them there would be completely unaware we'd ever been through the cistern and the tunnels surrounding it. The craftsmanship was what astounded me the most about the place; it was impossible not to notice.

"Dwarves and Ondi-Ne built this," Knight Vuller said, in awe. "Their friendship made them easy to hire by the Ava-Ondi who designed the high streets and the tower avenues."

"I think the humans are still a little sore about being enslaved for quarrying and hauling rock, mind you," Kovak added. "I know I would be."

"Well, we're in a uniquely advantaged position, going after a Prince no one seems to like the idea of," Gronin whispered.

I enjoyed inspecting the tall arches overhead, walking along brick paths that led us through a cistern the size of a small lake. "I still can't believe all this is suspended above the Capital."

"I forgot, Ondi-Ne aren't typically fond of heights," Gronin said. "The idea of you being so high up for so long must have been maddening."

"Not at all, we like heights," Riv said.

"Speak for yourself," I replied. "Put some nice dirt under my feet, a tree within reach, and all's right with the world. I try not to think about how precarious this place truly is."

"You'd know, master of stone," Kovak muttered.

"I do!" I whispered in acknowledgement. "You wouldn't believe the secrets these stones tell, and what understanding how they're stacked to make this place can do to your sense of peace. All these arches, reaching for each other, connecting, those supports we just passed, even the way the bricks are laid together in the floor – if it isn't all done just right, this entire cistern, the aqueducts, the houses and street above, would collapse under the pressure of wind blowing in the wrong direction. It may take a few years, you know, but it would happen just the same."

"Never, this place is as hard and sturdy as a mountain," Kovak said.

"He's right," Nurn said, "All things are placed in such a way so the stones press against each other, keeping a balance. Lesser craftsmen would not have been able to build this to last through an age. You only have to look at the Ruins of Dower Street in the south to see how much work it takes to bring a place like this down."

"That was destroyed by dragons," Kovak said. "Not bad construction."

"That's how they brought it down, boy. They ripped the right supports out from under it, and down it went. Not easy for the likes of us, but those were centuries-old dragons, with talons as long as you are tall."

"Wish I could have seen that," Kovak said.

"You and me both," Riv said.

"The gate is down there," I said. "Hold a moment, there's a ward ahead." The ward was a circle of writing on one of the larger supports. I'd known about it for weeks. Unlike the other, invisible wards, this one was made with golden lettering and enchanted by Chonolo himself. It and the King were connected; he would know if someone was on their way through the palace's Low Gate. I reached out to the stone upon which the ward was written, Oroza could sense everything I was doing, and he waited to add his unique energy to mine.

A pebble dropped in the water on the opposite side of the pillar, and I felt Riv snap one of his shadow rods and move away from us. There was nothing to see. I mentally felt around the space and saw nothing out of place. I also couldn't find out how a pebble was knocked off one of the walkways into the water; the stone only knew it moved, nothing more.

Kovak followed Riv's example while the others drew weaponry. "Spread out, stay on this side of the pillar," Gronin ordered quietly. "What are you feeling here?" he asked me.

"A pebble moved on its own," I told him.

"Be ready," Gronin said, drawing his thick bladed swords.

I concentrated on silencing the ward on the opposite side of the pillar, and was disappointed to learn that it had been created by a much more talented mind. The ward could see what was in front of it, feel vibrations, and sense the auras of anything that passed in front, and it faced the only tunnel leading into the palace from the cistern. "This is more difficult than I thought," I said.

I could feel a small fallen piece of brick scrape across the stone path in front of me, and Vuller pushed me off the walkway. I felt the vibrations of something striking the stone through the water as I was emerging. I was astounded as my vision cleared to see the Crusher Duke, who appeared as if from thin air, take a downward swing at Vuller, who barely spun out of the way. The impact of his heavily gauntleted fist broke ancient brick, sending fragments of the path spinning across the water.

Even to an Ondi's senses, Carmack was fast. Those dreadful weighted gauntlets didn't seem to slow him down. Vuller was well trained, and quite quick herself, spinning backwards and slashing at the Crusher Duke with her double-headed handaxes. It barely slowed him down, but I could see her intention. Vuller was drawing the Crusher Duke to one of the broader platforms in the cistern, where stone paths crossed and the knights could surround him. The water of the cistern was deep; no one could fight while they were off the stone paths.

I glanced at Oroza, who snapped his own shade rod and disappeared. I was about to do the same when I sensed something for the very first time. There was a human practitioner in the cistern with us, and he was using a type of flesh manipulating magic that I'd never seen before. I didn't have enough time to interact with the weave he was crafting so I could counteract it, or force the energy to dissipate, or to find the magician, until it was too late.

Just as Vuller was taking her last steps back towards the larger platform, she fell. "I can't move my legs!" she shouted, pulling herself back with her arms as quickly as she could.

Before anyone could reach her and pull her onto the platform, the Crusher Duke said, "I'm sorry," and lived up to his namesake. One of his broad weighted gauntlets punched her upper chest and helmet, and I could hear her armour crack. His right fist came down hard enough to violently shake the brick path as I tried to climb out of the water.

"Riv! Get to it!" I shouted the instant before I snapped my shade rod, and finished climbing out of the water. Only my shadow, a flickering shape in the inconsistent amber light of the cistern, was visible, but I could feel that other magician searching for me.

Gronin had sheathed his swords and switched to a heavy hammer called Thuun, a beast of a weapon that belonged to his grandfather. The man was agile with the weapon, keeping it moving, dodging the Crusher Duke's swings until he was able to meet the flat face of the man's fist with a hammer blow that made the air shudder.

The opening was enough for Kovak to attempt a slashing attack from the rear, looking to open the back of the giant human's knee. A push of water and air swept him off his feet and off the stone platform, and by that act, I found my opponent, the human magician. I stuck my hand in my pocket and retrieved several pebbles, which I tossed towards the stone arches above. I grasped them with my mind and sent them spinning through the air at blazing speed towards the human mage. As they struck him faster than arrows, I focused my will. The air was filled with the sound of thunder as one of my enchanted pebbles transmogrified from dense stone to air, exploding in an instant.

The shield that kept my opponent invisible to the eye took most of the impact, but he was sent off his feet, and crashed into a support post. The man, with a long, dark beard and solid features, regarded me from black eyes as he stood. "Your people killed my master. I'm going to strip you of your flesh, child."

That was the first time I met Charthanga, the one who would later become the Cinder Lord. Our rivalry began there, and though it cooled for a time, it would eventually tear the countryside apart. There are things in the grimoire I studied that are not normally taught to students. Only masters with good moral thinking should know them, and to those people, that sort of magic is of little interest.

"You underestimate me," I told Charthanga. I was an adolescent on a revenge quest; that dangerous part of my people's grimoire was fascinating, and, more importantly, useful. "You will know suffering," I told him.

I raised my hand as though gripping his front teeth and found purchase on them with my mind. All his defences were broken, thanks to my previous attack. He screamed as I chipped the same letters I'd carved into my explosive pebbles into one of them. Before he could counter, I focused my will to a fine point and forced one of his front teeth to become air and fire in an instant. To any onlooker it looked like a violent explosion. The subtlety was lost on everyone who was uneducated in magic, but I remember feeling a twisted sense of satisfaction as Charthanga collapsed.

His face, his mouth especially, was a ruined, charred mess. He was still alive, breathing through his ruined, ragged flesh, but I did not expect that he would live long. He gurgled and struggled with his breathing. I could feel his mind breaking under the pressure of pain and rage.

I had overestimated myself, in truth. If I had transmogrified his entire front tooth into flame, he wouldn't have a head left. I had, in reality, done so to a tiny sliver of that tooth; it was enough to ruin him for the rest of that battle, but he would survive. He would summon dragons who had no place in this reality, he would conduct the Cinder War, and he would be instrumental in the destruction of this world.

"Naze!" Gronin shouted. "Rakiz is here!"

I turned towards him, where he was narrowly dodging the Crusher Duke. Nurn was charging at the human from his left, swords poised to strike the giant in the ribs. I was just in time to see Gronin inexplicably disappear, and Nurn the Knight appear in his place directly in front of the Crusher Duke, who was in mid-swing. It was enough to make Nurn stumble, and to my surprise, the knight was able to put up both his hands and absorb a straight-on blow. His boots scraped along the bricks under the force of the punch, and for a heartbeat, the Crusher Duke looked surprised. Then he brought his other fist across with horrific speed.

Armour was crushed and bones were broken as Nurn was sent flying off the platform, stumbling over a walkway and falling into the water. The high magic was enough for me to feel Rakiz there, and I read the stone paths with my mind. The magic she used was powerful enough for her aura to surge, and the stones felt that.

I pulled a flattened pebble with my mark on it and tossed it over where I suspected she was standing. She noticed, and tried to grip my skin. I could see the weave of magic trying to tear it away from my flesh and with no little effort I countered just enough. I was sure of where she was then, and my pebble had landed on the platform just behind her.

I lowered my shoulder and braced myself as I connected myself to the symbol on the flat pebble, and I was drawn down the walkway, skipping across the water, then onto the platform in an instant. It wasn't teleportation, but in that moment, it was exactly what I needed: a high speed charge that sent me colliding through Rakiz, even though she was invisible until the moment I made contact. It wasn't perfect, but it was enough to send her off the platform, to distract her, and I was on my feet.

"You idiot!" Gronin shouted as he put himself between me and the Crusher Duke, who took great strides to close the distance between us on the platform. I'd gotten too close to the Crusher, and if it weren't for Gronin landing a lucky strike on the Crusher's elbow in mid-swing, I would have been made one with the stone in a very abrupt way.

For the first time since the conflict began, I heard Carmack, the Crusher Duke, cry out in pain. That was Riv's time, and I hoped with all my being that he was where he had to be. My prayer was answered. My brother appeared atop the Crusher Duke! He used the strap of his shoulder guard to swing towards Carmack's left wrist, and he stuck one of his broader knives down his gauntlet, slicing and slashing and ripping the flesh of the man's wrist.

Rakiz rose from the water then, and she attempted to strike at me with a burst of steam and fire. I attempted to block it, drawing the cool water from behind me into a chilling veil, and managed to do so, a proud instant wherein I demonstrated an exceptional level of focus and speed.

Then the sounds of my brother screaming broke through the self-satisfied instant. Rakiz had fooled me, and changed the direction of her furious assault. I let my barrier of water drop as I attempted to interrupt the furious magic that Rakiz inflicted upon my brother, who was enveloped first in steam, then in bare flame as she flayed him alive. I'll never forget the grin on her face as the air was filled with the sounds of his screams and the smell of his burning flesh.

The Crusher Duke took two long strides towards her and swung both his fists down, howling with rage and anguish. The impact was enough to utterly destroy Rakiz, who didn't realize that Riv had already accomplished his mission, to cut her mark from flesh, the mark that allowed her to control the Crusher Duke for nearly two decades. He fell to his knees in front of the ruin that was once her body and beat the bricks until Gronin laid a hand on his shoulder. "You're with us again, my old friend."

The Crusher Duke wept deeply.

I rushed to my brother. Oroza was already there, lifting his charred hand, holding it in his small clutches. The amount of healing magic the dragon focused on that body was awe-inspiring, and I joined him in trying to bring my brother back at first, but there was no saving him. There are some unnatural deaths that ensure the door to return is forever locked. Rakiz had that kind of power, and she used it on him.

My brother Riv, who had many times been a source of irritation, but was equally a wonderful entertainer to me, and another perspective I'd learned to take for granted. He was a partner for my entire life until then, my twin, and the other half of my soul. He was gone.

Kovak and Nurn were within the range of Oroza's healing power, and they rose without injury, joining us on the platform. I felt the healing energy begin to affect Charthanga, and put a hand on Oroza's head, gently stroking the smooth scales. "You must stop now," I whispered. "Guards are coming, and he'll never return to us."

Oroza knew, and he stopped, and then he crawled into the front of my robe where he wept for days.

Weeks later, the Crusher Duke, Gronin, Nurn, Oroza, Kovak, and all of the Draconian Guardians assassinated the Prince, leaving evidence that Riv stole the Enduring Light, and that he was the true assassin. They used his knives for the grisly work, sparing no guard, no servant, or other witness who could say they were there. When it was done, they made sure Minstrels and Criers alike were giving Riv the bloody credit. The Goblin, the Slasher, the Ondi-Ne who wanted nothing more than revenge, and with no grave or shrine, he would forever be that frightening shade, that murderer of Princes.

I incinerated my brother, and scattered his ashes across the ruins of the High Temple that once stood where my refuge was built. He is in the foundations of this place, something only Kovak knew when we laid the first stones.

Chapter XXIV

"Many of you know what I'll be doing next," Naze said as he gripped Doril's hand. Sweat was running down his face, and the effort of keeping the power from the Enduring Light from overwhelming him, of keeping his thoughts in order, was almost more than he could bear.

"I can see three portals, all standing at the edge of opposing cosmic forces: a sun being born, another collapsing, and another singing the song of creation as it stands between the other two like a fountain of endless light. That is the secret of the Enduring Light; it stands in the crux of perfect balance, between destruction, genesis, and the force of the cycle. There is no greater power, and I am fortunate that it was near during my worst moment, the instant of my brother's death."

"You can stop speaking," Lizabe told him. "Perform your masterwork, we know what comes next."

"No, I need to finish sorting this out for myself, because if I'm wrong..." Naze closed his eyes and struggled to hold the power within himself. "If I'm wrong, I have to die and take this with me so you can all find another way to correct the mess I've made of this place."

"Then tell us, old friend," Kovak said.

"The Prince was right there, hiding. He was Rakiz's pupil, and he had the Enduring Light, only feet away, and he redoubled his efforts to stay hidden when she was killed. This bauble was in his hand, he'd finally noticed it. Now I can connect the two points of power through time, and send one thought to myself at the right moment. That one thought will change the catastrophic events that come after. It will put me on a new path starting in that moment of my youth - a path that is not guided by revenge and grief, one that may allow for forgiveness, and may even lead back to my people, to my old master. It just takes one thought. I can make this world the place it should have been."

"Stop! No one can know what kind of change that will bring!" cried a voice from the audience, but Naze could not make out who, his vision was failing already. The light within was too bright for him to see anything outside of himself.

"By grace, I love the world, I love you people," were the last words he said before he forced his entire consciousness through the Enduring Light, and all his will, his entire being, was reduced down to one thought that his younger self would be forced to have at just such a time.

* * *

Naze pulled a flattened pebble with his sorcerer's mark on it and tossed it over where he suspected Rakiz was standing. She noticed, and tried to grip his skin. He could see the weave of magic trying to tear it away from his flesh, and with no little effort he countered it just enough, twisting the strands of power out of shape. He was sure of where she was then, and his pebble had landed on the platform well past her.

Naze lowered his shoulder and braced himself as he connected to the symbol on the flat pebble, and he was drawn down the walkway, then sent skipping across the water on quick feet, then onto Rakiz in an instant. It wasn't teleportation, but in that moment it was exactly what he needed, a high-speed charge that sent him colliding through her. The moment he made contact, Rakiz became visible to everyone. It wasn't perfect, but it was enough to send her off the platform, to distract her, and he was still on his feet when the act was done.

"You idiot!" Gronin shouted as he put himself between Naze and the Crusher Duke, who took great strides to close the distance between them on the platform. He'd gotten too close to the Crusher, and if it weren't for Gronin landing a lucky strike on the Crusher's elbow in mid-swing, he would have been made one with the stone in a very abrupt way.

For the first time since the conflict began, they heard Carmack, the Crusher Duke, cry out in pain. That was Riv's cue. The quick Ondi-ne appeared atop the Crusher Duke! He used the strap of his shoulder guard to swing towards Carmack's left wrist, and he stuck one of his broader knives down his gauntlet, slicing and slashing and ripping the flesh of the man's wrist.

Naze heard a crack in his mind, as though a barrier had been broken, and found himself looking towards his brother, realizing with crystal clarity that everything depended on Riv releasing the Crusher Duke from Rakiz's magical control. If anything interfered, all would be lost.

Naze focused and did his best to create a barrier around Riv that could protect him against most magical attacks. It was weak, early magic that he'd learned when he was younger, and he wished he spent much more time studying the grimoire's more passive, protective spells instead of delving into the offensive magical knowledge.

Gronin moved between Naze and the Crusher Duke, who was ineffectively trying to shake Riv off. Everyone still on their feet recognized what Riv was doing, and stood back, hoping.

Naze saw Rakiz begin rising from the water just to his left, right next to him. She would try to stop Riv; the protective barrier would not hold against her. Gronin wouldn't have time to turn and swing at her, leaving Naze only one option. He dug into his pocket and retrieved most of the stones he'd marked with explosive air and fire runes. He pitched the lot of them into the water atop her head and shoulders, and with a degree of wilful force previously unknown to him, he turned them into flame and air.

He felt her, the stone of the platform, and the cistern around her shatter brutally before they were all sent into the water by the concussion of the explosion. Naze only felt a flash of heat and pressure.

* * *

Light and heat and the loving will of another infused him from the core outward. Naze had never felt more wanted in his life, and when he opened his eyes, it was to Oroza gripping his hand. Healing energy was pouring out of the dragonling. "I'm alive," Naze said. "By your glory, I'm alive."

Oroza collapsed onto his chest, and that was when Naze noticed burns on his robe.

"Maybe a little more practice before you try that again?" Riv said, clutching his hand. "You were a little too close."

"I'm sorry," Naze said.

"Don't do it again," Riv told him. "Don't know what I'd do without you, Brother."

"If it weren't for my armour, I don't think I would have fared any better," Gronin said. The cloth covering his armour plates was a torn mass, hanging by threads.

Naze got up gently, and then saw the Crusher Duke, sitting beside the corpse of the Prince.

"The boy just appeared after Rakiz was killed. He rushed the platform," Riv said, gesturing towards what remained of the Prince. "Carmack thanked me, put me down behind him and, before the Prince could finish raising his hands to do whatever magic he thought he was about to use, Carmack hit him. Never seen anything like it," Riv whispered. "Crusher Duke turned him into broken bones and paste in three hits. Think this kingdom is up for grabs now."

"King's dead," Carmack said, slowly rising to his feet. "That Prince was learning to animate him from Chonolo, so he could appear to be coughing and sputtering in his bed when servants were allowed to clean his chambers once a week. Kept the rumour of life alive. Don't know who killed him originally, though."

Beside the Prince's remains was a dull looking piece of crystal in the shape of a teardrop. Kovak picked it up, and Naze was immediately seized by a sense of nervousness. "May I see that, please?" he asked urgently.

"Sure, looks like it needs a polish though," Kovak said.

"We should get going, guards will be on their way," Carmack, the Crusher Duke said.

"You're all right, old friend?" Gronin asked.

"I barely remember much of what I've done, but I know enough," Carmack said, nodding. "I'll be all right. Better when I've returned to the north. I wonder if my father still lives."

"Lord Kuderin?" Nurn said as he tried to re-affix the armour on his shoulder. "He'll outlive us all, that old bear."

"You're right," Carmack said, smiling. "I owe you a debt, goblin," he said to Riv.

"I take coinage in lieu of gratitude," Riv replied with a grin. "Or vanilla spirits."

"I'll see you have both," he said. Then he turned to Naze, who was examining the crystal. "So, what is it, Master Naze?"

"Anything special in there?" Kovak.

"There was," Naze said. "But it's an empty vessel now."

"So, not dangerous?" Kovak asked, extending his hand.

"No," Naze said, handing it to him.

In the next instant, Kovak dropped it to the bricks beneath his feet, and crushed the bauble. "Now we know for sure, I suppose," said a strong voice from a few feet down a darkened path. "The Prince was a true novice, and his master was a fool."

"Who are you?" Naze asked.

"Charthanga. Your brother knows me well enough. I granted him mercy, not knowing that your people would kill my master not long after." He looked at the gathered company and shook his head. "I am no contest for your company, and I suppose I should thank you for your mercy, but you've made refugees of everyone who survived our duel. The Royal Family is dead, there is no point in risking life or limb avenging them, so I'll repay your kindness by telling the guards I ran you off, that you took a secret passage down to the city below."

"Thank you," Naze said.

"Don't," Charthanga said, this time at the pace of an Ondi-Ne. "You don't realize the loss I'm suffering. I am displaced. The only difference between you and me is that your wandering begins right now, while mine begins before the dawn. You will be accused of killing a Prince, and I'll suffer the same penalty for failing to defend him if I'm caught. Go, and pray you don't cross me under different circumstances."

"We take our leave," Riv said, nodding at everyone. "Yes?"

"Run," Kovak agreed.

"I'll be right behind," Gronin said. He walked to where Vuller's body lay, followed by Carmack, and Nurn.

"I'm so sorry," Carmack said.

"You weren't in control," Gronin replied as he carefully retrieved a necklace from her body. The silver oval was decorated with a golden hand holding up three fingers. "The Treble House amulet. Her people will want this returned."

"You won't go alone," Carmack said.

"She was a great knight," Nurn said. "Her people will know it, I'll make sure I'm there in person to help you tell her story."

"And you, Naze? It's toward the coast. You, your brother, and your dragon would be in good company," Gronin said.

"We'll join you," Naze said without hesitation.

"But now, we run, right?" Riv said, nodding his head frantically. If that wasn't enough, the sounds of guards' boots echoing across the vaulted cistern certainly was, and the company made haste.

"Did he just call me a dragon? I'm only a dragonling, you know," Oroza said sleepily from within what was left of the front of Naze's robes.

"Any dragonling who can perform miracles is a full-fledged dragon, in my eye," Gronin said.

"Absolutely," Naze agreed.

"Thank you," Oroza said as he stretched his neck so he could see. "Only, walk more gracefully, or this dragon will sick up."

Illustrations

Thank you for reading.

What follows are illustrations
drawn by Marcus Froment.

189

Thank you so much for purchasing the printed version of Brightwill. My dream of writing for a living is made possible by readers like you. To find out more about Brightwill and my other, please visit:

www.randolphlalonde.com

Other Novels By Randolph Lalonde

Spinward Fringe Broadcast 0: Origins
Spinward Fringe Broadcast 1 & 2: Resurrection & Awakening
Spinward Fringe Broadcast 3: Triton
Spinward Fringe Broadcast 4: Frontline
Spinward Fringe Broadcast 5: Fracture
Spinward Fringe Broadcast 6: Fragments
The Expendable Few: A Spinward Fringe Novel
Spinward Fringe Broadcast 7: Framework
Spinward Fringe Broadcast 8: Renegades

www.ingramcontent.com/pod-product-compliance
Lightning Source LLC
Chambersburg PA
CBHW021147130626
46554CB00005B/1705